Boychick

To RN the only begettor

"Beas Tristant, curtois Tristant
Tun cors, ta vie a de commant!"

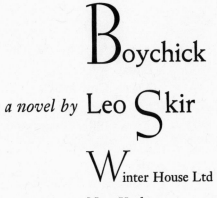

# Boychick

*a novel by* Leo Skir

Winter House Ltd
New York 1971

# Boychick

WILLE GE BEOH BESWUNGEN on leonunge? Would ye be whipped in order to learn?

This from Aelfric's *Colloquy*, which I had been studying, or rather, taking, as part of my Old English course. I was doing what all students do with language courses—leaving it to the last.

In my lap was the Gottfried von Strassburg *Tristan*, just come out as Penguin paperback.

It is Thanksgiving Day and I home with my parents, Mama and Papa Tsalis.

"Leo," Mama says, "take a piece of bread and soak up the rest of your gravy."

She hesitates a second but, unable to control herself, takes a piece of bread and soaks it in my plate-gravy and hands it to me.

"Please dear," says my father, "he's a grown boy."

Indeed, such is the case. I am twenty-eight.

I glance at my watch.

"I must leave soon," I said, "I have a lot of studying to do."

"Can't you study here?" Mama says. "You know how happy it makes us. I wish you would sleep over sometime. You don't know how happy it makes me to think my boy is sleeping in the next room."

"Do you want to speak with me before you leave?" Dad says, winking.

"You know I do," I say.

We go into his room where he sits at his desk and takes out his checkbook, and a few moments later I am holding a hundred dollar check which is for my food and other expenses for the next month.

Mama comes into the room.

"Look at your shoes," she says. "I'm ashamed you should go around wearing shoes like that."

I look at the shoes, which are sort of falling to pieces. I had bought a new pair but they had hurt.

"The known evil is better than the unknown evil," I tell her, wondering who will shame me. My neighbors? My fellow-students at NYU?

"Promise me you'll buy shoes tomorrow," she says.

"I'll buy shoes tomorrow," I say.

"I was going to buy shoes tomorrow for myself," she says, "but I feel that I can do without a new pair of shoes as long as I know my son is wearing a new pair of shoes."

And then, when Dad was driving me to the subway, it happened, as it always happened, one of these peculiar conversations that make me feel so bad for such a long time afterward.

"What are you planning to do next term?" Dad says (as if he doesn't know).

"I've got a residency in that writers' colony upstate," I said.

"You know," Dad says, "I've got the money now for you to go to school next term, but I won't be able to send you to school later."

I sit, looking out the window, wondering why the money that is available now for next term could not be put away until later when I had returned to the city. But I could not ask. It was as if this were part of the rules, that Daddy's gold, like faery gold, could not stay the term's absence and that I could not ask it to.

We were at the subway station.

"Well," Dad says, "think about it."

Which thinking does not come. There seem to be no alternatives, but only a picture of my father taking his money away like a child removing his bills (paper, counterfeit) from under his edge of the Monopoly board.

Which thoughts of Monopoly come to me more strongly since I am now sitting on the train which is moving on elevated tracks so that there is below the vista of small private houses with sloping rooftops, looking like the tiny colored wood-block houses of Monopoly.

The Gottfried von Strassburg *Tristan* lay in my lap. As always after a visit home, it was impossible for me to read. Literature had no meaning. That Tristan's mouth was red, his arms and hands shapely and dazzling white, what could all of this matter?

I could almost hear my father's voice saying, "What does it get you?"—see the shrug of his shoulders.

Tristan's arm could only be important if it had to be

remembered for a college examination.

An arm, its beauty, the discussion of the same, he would have regarded as frivolous. An infected or broken arm, on the contrary, would be a subject for discussion. Medicine, treatment, Blue Cross policies were the great objective realities.

Beauty, perfection, like happiness and singing—all were beyond his spectrum.

Feeling the one hundred dollar check in my pocket, I felt ashamed of my disloyalty.

Opening to page ninety-five, which was my place, I read:

" 'Dear Father' asked Tristan, 'What is the matter? Where have your good looks gone?'

" 'You took them from me, my son.' "

"Each bulb," I thought, "gives rise to another bulb, but there's always a flower in between."

I decided to swim at the St. George.

At De Kalb Avenue I got out and walked past the lighted Nedicks and frankfurter stands.

I walked six blocks and came to a corner. There was a thoroughfare. To my right was a new municipal building, very fascist-looking, smooth, monolithic frònt. All around cars seemed to whizz in the early evening light.

Standing there, oddly abstracted, almost hypnotized, I had a vision of myself, years later, standing, for some reason, on an expanse of raised highway (why I on foot and all these cars whizzing by?). I could see the pink of the sunrise, the railing painted green.

Then the moment and the vision were over.

At the St. George, I paid for the pool and went in.

The pool was not crowded and I was able to swim several

lengths. After about half an hour I got out and went into the steam room.

There is a notice outside the steam room that bathing suits are to be worn and no soap used inside, but a fat, ugly man, naked and middle-aged, was standing in the steam room soaping himself.

Sitting almost directly in front of him was a young Negro boy, goodlooking, who seemed to be waiting for him.

"Here," said the fat man. "Soap my back."

He extended the soap to the Negro boy.

The boy just looked down, embarrassed.

"He's afraid someone will think he's a *faggot*," said the fat man.

No one in the steam room (there were about eight other people) looked at him or said anything.

I got up and went to the showers but not before the fat man had made the faggot remark again. He was very ugly.

While I was taking a shower I noticed a blond boy outside the shower stalls. He looked about fourteen or fifteen. He was, it seemed to me, looking at me.

Drying his cock, he waved it up and down like a railway switch signal.

"Now, Leo," I said to myself, "*that* is a boy. You have a bad mind."

He was gone when I left the showers, but when I went to my locker I saw him again. He was wearing his shorts (boxer) and combing his hair. He was putting a wave (breaking) in the front.

It seemed to me that he was looking at me.

Later Boychick told me I had looked very frightened.

When he sat down on the long bench it was with his back to me. He sat so close I could feel the presence of his body, even its heat.

He turned and said something to me but I didn't catch it. When I stood up to put on my shirt, he was already dressed and re-combing his hair. But now he was, unmistakably, looking directly at me. Like Donne says, our eyebeams twisted and did thread our eyes.

Wow!

I stared at him. Was he a psychopath of some sort, a prostitute, a blackmailer? He didn't look like any of these things. If anything, he looked so terribly open-faced and baby-like that I wondered if I was mistaken.

Then Boychick raised his eyebrows in question and I knew I wasn't.

I tapped my forehead to show that I was thinking and continued to dress.

My heart was pounding terribly.

Then he turned and left.

I grabbed my coat and followed him up the steps and out onto the street. He had not turned to look at me. I wondered if he knew I was behind him.

When we were outside I said, "Hey wait! You didn't give me a chance to tie my shoelaces. Hold my jacket for a second."

He stood there, staring at me, a half-angry stare, and I wondered if he was going to hold the jacket. Then he took it, and I stooped over to tie the shoelaces, asking, when I was down there (and looking at his shoes, which were very new and very polished), "How old are you?"

"Sixteen," he said.

I got up.

"Do you have any cigs?" he said.

"No," I said, "but I can get some."

"I'll wait outside," he said.

This brought to mind again the suspicion that he did not want to be seen with me now so that later he could deny knowing me.

When I came out with the cigarettes, he said, "Do you want to go into that bar?"

He motioned to the bar across the street.

He meant, of course, to go into the bar in order to make out in the men's room.

"No," I said, "I'd like to go someplace where we can lie down."

"I have to be in the subway by eleven," he said.

"I live all the way uptown in Manhattan," I said, "and I've got a landlady. Look, we can go to the house of a friend of mine." Alys didn't have her phone in yet. I couldn't call. I hoped she would be home.

Boychick puffed his cigarette.

"Is it much of a ride?" he said.

"No," I said, "It's on the Lower East Side in Manhattan. We can use the IND."

We started to walk toward the Jay Street station.

"Let's smoke one more cigarette before we get into the subway," I said.

We were now at the subway entrance. A bus came to the corner.

"That's the bus I use to get home," said Boychick. "It takes over half an hour. What's your name?"

"Leo," I said. "Leo Tsalis. And yours?"

"Leroy," he said. "I don't like to give people my last name."

"You don't have to," I said. "I've lived until now without your last name."

"I just don't want you to think it's just you," he said.

"I don't." I said.

I had finished my cigarette. There was no reason for further delay. We had by now walked up and down the block three times.

"I think I should tell you," I said, "that my interest in the subject has been almost academic."

Boychick puffed his cigarette in grownup style.

"What do you mean by that?" he said.

"I mean," I said, "I've never really made it with guys. Let's go."

We went into the subway.

W<small>HOSE HOUSE</small> are we going to?" said Boychick, this on the subway platform.

"It's the house of a friend of mine," I said. "A girl."

I noticed the look of surprise on Boychick's face.

"A girl?" he said. "Does she know?"

"What?" I said.

"About—us," he said.

"Well," I said, "she will when I tell her."

"She won't be angry?" said Boychick.

"Angry?" I said. "She'll be very happy."

"Is she your sister?" he said.

"No," I said, "I don't have a sister."

"My sister lives in the Village," he said. "She's got a furnished room with her roommate. They have a hi-fi set and Ahmad Jamal records. And we smoke marijuana and drink Thunderbirds. Have you ever drunk Thunderbirds?"

"No," I said.

"They're great," he said. "They make you feel so dizzy."

"I think the marijuana helps too," I said.

Our train came in.

"Are you a rebel?" he asked.

This startled me, since I, born in 1932, associated the word rebel with those holding the gates of Madrid.

"What do you mean?" I said.

"Are you a beatnik?" he said.

"No," I said. "Not really."

Boychick's face fell.

"The girl we're going to is the girlfriend of one of the leading beat poets," I said.

I named him.

"Have you heard of him?" I said.

"No," said Boychick. "Is *she* a beatnik?"

"They don't call themselves beatniks," I said. "But she is."

"Is she pretty?" he said.

"No," I said. "She's got acne. Her face looks like boiling vegetable soup with all the alphabet noodles. She's a lesbian."

"My sister hangs out with a lesbian beatnik crowd," he said. "Have you been to the Café Bizarre?"

"No," I said.

"What's her name?" he said. "The girl we're going to?"

"Alys," I said (not spelling it out so that it sounded like a normal Alice), "Alys Kagen."

"Do you fight with your parents?" he said.

Now I realized his definition of rebel.

"Yes," I said, "all the time."

He shook his head like a kid in a high school play coming on stage with charcoal smudges on his face to indicate a battle-weary GI.

"My parents are too much." he said.

"What do they do?" I said.

"They make me dress up all the time," he said. "Just like I was a dummy or monkey or something. My father's always wanting to show me off. He's a union official and makes me go to all the receptions dressed up in a tuxedo. Just like a little monkey."

We changed trains and got out at Second Avenue. The station, as always, stank of urine.

The part of the East Side at which we had gotten out was once wholly Jewish and now almost entirely Puerto Rican.

We passed the vestigial remains of the Jewish period, the still-open ritual baths, the candy stores, a store selling tombstones, MITSVOT, with Hebrew lettering, and several synagogues.

Alys had moved here because Allen had his apartment here. And why had Allen moved here? It seemed to be a not unpleasant romantic notion, almost like a leftover from an old Clifford Odets play, to want to live in this poverty-stricken street with its cockroaches and rats. My grandfather (may he rest in peace), whose name was my name, Leo— I being named after him since he died before I was born (Jews do not name a child for a living relative)—my grandfather Leo had lived in a basement until he died, his explanation having been that he never wanted, if his fortunes were reversed, to move down.

"I don't know if Alys is in," I told Boychick. "She doesn't have a phone so I couldn't call her."

"It's OK," Boychick said.

It was then (or was it before, when we were at the subway entrance?) that I told him that I didn't have much money. I even told him how much cash I had on me. It was less than two dollars. I even told him what my monthly allowance was, that I had about three dollars a day to live on.

"It's OK," said Boychick. "I don't take money."

Alys's apartment was on 2nd Street. No one was home. I had hoped that even if Alys was out Joycelyn her roommate would be there. Joycelyn *was* pretty, which might interest Boychick, although her beauty was so close to his that I wasn't sure. She was one of those handsome gentiles: blonde, with white skin and pink cheeks, like Boychick.

But there was no one at home. Our only chance was that Allen or Peter would be home. Their apartment was only a block away.

We walked over but no one was in.

I felt like a mariner on the sea hitting a calm or contrary wind.

"It's all right," Boychick said.

"Would you like to go to a dairy restaurant?" I said. "You can have strawberry shortcake."

"All right," he said.

While we were walking to the restaurant he talked about his sex life.

"Does your sister know you're making it with guys?" I said.

"No!" he said. "I make it with her girlfriends. I just ask her for the key and we go and make it. It's a little embarrassing until you start kissing."

"Are you going to tell your sister about the guys?" I said.

"I don't know," he said. "I guess so. Soon. All my sister's friends are lesbians. Have you ever seen two girls making love?"

"No." I said.

"It's the most beautiful thing in the world," he said. "If I could paint, that's the thing I would paint."

"You could get a polaroid camera," I said. And then I was angry at myself for such a coarse remark. But Boychick smiled as though I'd said something very funny. He had a sweet smile.

At Ratner's I ordered a shortcake and coffee for Boychick, just coffee for myself. I was too excited to eat.

The strawberry shortcake at Ratner's is an odd Jewish idea of strawberry shortcake. It's a layer cake really, not a shortcake, the layers made of whipped cream and strawberries, with a small pitcher of strawberry syrup on the side to pour over the cake.

Boychick finished the cake and lapped up the syrup. "I shouldn't be eating this," he said. "At school, in gym, they gave me a special diet."

I hadn't noticed any particular fatness about Boychick.

We walked back along Second Avenue to the subway, passing the delicacy shops with their barrels of pickles, mounds of Hopjes, strings of bagels.

I looked at Boychick, wondering if he had been in the neighborhood before and if he found it interesting. It was impossible to tell. He simply exhibited the eagerness of a dog being taken for a walk.

In Ratner's we had talked about heroin. He had told me that his mother had found some on his clothes. She had told his father, who had taken him to the police station.

"I told them I hadn't been taking it," he said. "I said you can't hold me. I'm under eighteen. You can strip me, search me, you won't find any marks on me. My father got frightened. He gave the police twenty dollars to forget it. He's such a four-flusher. He thinks we're so hot."

"Are you on probation," I asked.

"No!" he said. "I'm careful. I never took any of the stuff when I was carrying it."

"Are you carrying any now?" I said.

"Are you kidding?" he said.

"Are you?" I said.

"No," he said.

"How much money do you have now?" I said.

"Here," he said, "hold out your hand."

I held out my hand and felt metal in my palm.

"What is it?" I said.

"My keys," he said.

"Don't you have a cent?" I said.

"Nope," he said.

I wondered whether I had given him a token when we came uptown in the subway but I couldn't remember.

"Did you pay for the pool?" I said.

"No," he said. "I have a school pass."

I wondered if the school pass was a reduction or let the student in for nothing, but I didn't ask. We walked along in silence for a space.

We came to First Avenue. The place where the Italians played *bocce* each Sunday now lay vacant.

As we crossed the street, Peter, Allen's roommate, came out of the subway.

"Oh, Peter," I said. "I'm so glad to see you! Alys wasn't in and my friend and I wanted to use her apartment. Can we stay with you, just for a few minutes? My friend Leroy can only stay for fifteen minutes. He has to be in the subway by eleven."

We began to walk with them back to 2nd Street. Peter was looking straight in front of him.

"What do you want to do?" he said.

"You know what we want to do," I said.

"No," he said. "What?"

"Screw," I said.

Actually, I had not discussed the matter with Boychick and was not at all sure what we were going to do or try to do but I found that now that things seemed to be working out I was almost half-coming in my pants.

Then I began to talk, rapidly, wildly, from embarrassment and the heat of expectation. I said—which was of course the wrong thing to say—that Boychick had been caught by the police carrying н.

At the corner, Peter stopped and said, "I've changed my mind. I think I'd like to be alone if you don't mind." And then, turning to Boychick, "Why don't you go over to Leo's place sometime. He has a nice apartment with a nice view. You ought to read Céline? Have you read Céline?"

"No," said Boychick.

"Well," said Peter, "you ought to. It's been nice meeting you."

He shook hands with Boychick.

Everything in me howled with frustration and shame.

"Oh Boychick!" I said. "I'm so sorry! I'm such a fool! It was my talking about the H that got him."

"It's all right," said Boychick.

"No, it isn't," I said.

"Do you have a TV set?" he said.

"No," I said.

"My father's always listening to TV," he said. "We gotta listen to whatever he wants to listen to. He's a real German. Did you ever see the Loretta Young Show?"

"No," I said.

He then went on to detail a story on the show that had starred Loretta Young, a story about a young girl who is able to tell what time it is, to the second, without a watch. He told it very well and, while he talked, I realized that he was really a very bright boy. It was true that he went to a technical high school, and also true that he did not have "cultural" interests. But his outline of the plot was as concise and clean as one could wish. No fellow student in my Chaucer class could have done as good a job on "The Knight's Tale."

He went on, seeing me preoccupied, I looking at the empty lot we were passing, a lot filled with broken bottles that reflected in the moonlight the pink and green neons of Katz's Delicatessen, I wondering if there was some basement doorway I could get Boychick into, he talking on about his high school. He didn't study much but could get anything memorized in

24

a few minutes. He went on to show me how good his memory was by naming the ways in which a feudal lord could acquire land. It was clear that they had come from an outline book with reasons (A) and (B).

He then began reciting some equations from his applied technology class, these being, it seemed, about electric current with the letter R standing for some unit of resistance.

I knew that he was talking in order to keep me from feeling bad. It was odd, he, so much younger, standing up under it better than I.

"I'm not so fascinated by technical devices," I said.

"Why not?" he said. "I think they're wonderful. Why, right over there—" he waved his arm at Katz's Delicatessen— "three hundred years ago there was nothing but cowboys and Indians."

I absorbed this knowledge in silence. There seemed to me nothing I could say.

At the subway entrance I took out all my money, which was now only some change, and gave him everything but thirty cents.

"This is all the money I have right now," I said. "I hope you don't think I'm being cheap."

"Oh, no," said Boychick. "I don't."

And then, standing there, he said, "Look, why don't you give me your name and address and I'll come over to your house tomorrow."

I stared at him.

"I've got to study tomorrow," I said.

"I mean, if you want to," he said.

"What time do you want to come?" I said.

"Around noon," he said. "I mean, that way we'd have more time. You wouldn't be so nervous."

"I don't think it's a good idea to leave my name and address around on paper," I said. "I mean—if your parents search your things."

"I'll memorize it and burn it up," he said.

"All right," I said. "Look, you won't mind if I leave you now? I'd like to go back and speak to Peter."

"No," he said. "I don't mind. I'll see you tomorrow then."

I wrote down my name and address and gave him the piece of paper, watching him hungrily as he went down the subway steps. I felt then that he might never come, and I never would have even felt him.

Peter was with Joycelyn when I went up to his apartment. I sat with them in the kitchen, facing the refrigerator on which was pasted a picture of Baudelaire.

Both Peter and Joycelyn were blond and from New Jersey, and both of Polish families. One would have taken them, both tall and blond, for brother and sister. They had been making it for about a year, Joycelyn having met Peter when he was alone, Allen having gone to a poet's conference in Peru.

I talked to them about Boychick.

"Why didn't you want him to come up?" I said. "Did you think he had any H on him?"

"No," said Peter, "I just didn't feel like company."

"Peter and Allen were picked up on Times Square the other night and searched," said Joycelyn, "and now that

Allen's coming out for marijuana on television he thinks the police may be watching the house and asked us to keep clean."

"Oh," I said.

"Why didn't you take the kid to your house?" said Peter.

"I told you," I said. "There wasn't time, and besides I was jumpy. I just didn't trust him."

"That's real skitsy," said Joycelyn, "you thinking the kid wanted to blackmail you or something. He's just an ordinary kid who wants to make it with you. That's very rough on him, all these skitsy thoughts."

"But he's still sixteen," I said, "*if* sixteen. I can get several years in jail for corrupting the morals of a minor."

"Who told you that?" said Joycelyn.

"A lawyer at a meeting of the Mattachine Society," I said. Joycelyn made a face.

"You shouldn't listen to him," she said, then adding, "—he shouldn't say things like that."

"But it happens to be the truth," I said.

"If you feel that way about it," said Peter, "why don't you make it platonic. You know, just a love affair?"

I looked past their blond heads at the picture of Baudelaire on the refrigerator.

Of course I didn't want no-hands with Boychick.

I stayed too long (as I always do when I feel I'm overstaying my welcome) and then I left. I walked across the Village to West 4th Street to take the AA train uptown. I had told Joycelyn I would write her if Boychick showed.

It had been windy earlier in the evening, but now the

calm that had preceded the wind recurred. It was an absolutely neutral night, and a stranger coming to the City would not have known what time of year it was.

I walked past NYU, now closed and unlighted, and past an automobile, one of those handpainted jobs so common in my youth, so seldom seen now, this one done in an odd blue color, the near-luminescent blue of the Movement shirts used by my Zionist group.

It seemed oddly ominous in the night.

I was home at a little after 1 a.m., took two sleeping pills and still found it hard to sleep. My heart was beating hard.

Next morning, in spite of the sleeping pills, which usually make me oversleep, I was up at six or seven, cleaning the apartment, taking down the garbage and wastepaper, and—as soon as it was nine and the Katzs downstairs were up—vacuuming the floors.

Then showering and going outside to cash my check and get food. If Boychick would be here at noon he would want to eat.

It was Friday and, somehow having a memory of him as Catholic, I bought fishcakes and spaghetti at Horn & Hardart. Also rum raisin ice cream.

I stopped at a pharmacy and bought some lubricant. And mouthwash, the mouthwash because I'd been told I had bad breath.

And then—it was already after eleven. I hurried to the bookstore at Broadway and 100th Street to try to get a copy of Bédier's *Tristan and Iseult*.

When we had been at Ratner's, Boychick had looked at my Tristan at one point, the Gottfried von Strassberg version. For some reason, his looking at it had made me very nervous.

It was too long for him, I told him, and the print was too small. I would get him another version.

"Give me some address that I can mail it to," I had said. We had not yet made an appointment to meet the next day. "If you don't want me to mail it to your home, I could mail it to you in care of your sister?"

Boychick had shaken his head. "Jesus, no! She'd be suspicious."

"I hate your not getting something I promised you," I said. "I know when I'm promised something and I don't get it— God!—I remember it longer than anything I do get."

"Don't worry," said Boychick. "I won't get mad."

It was then that we had arrived at the subway steps and seen Peter.

Now in the bright morning sunlight I ran to the bookstore.

They didn't have a copy of the *Tristan and Iseult* of Bédier.

I went home, shaved, took another shower.

It was now twenty to twelve. I put *Voi che sapete* on the phonograph.

Voi che sapete
che cosa e amor
Donne vedete
s'io l'ho nel cor.

You who know
what love is
Tell me if I have it
in my heart.

"He will not come," I said to myself. "Cherubino will not come."

But these words would not stop the hopes that loomed on every side of the emptiness like the walls of water of the Red Sea ready to rush in again upon the empty space I continued to cross.

"He will not come," I said aloud.

It was now twelve o'clock, but the hopes on each side mounted and swirled, not to be denied either their height or their power of crushing the hope that was left. No miracle could make them go away.

At twelve-thirty I sat down to write Joycelyn a postcard.

I put the postcard in the typewriter and typed out: *12:35. Boychick hasn't shown. . . .*

And, overcome by cramps of desire, with these words I went in and masturbated until I was covered with sweat. I took another shower, trying to cool my throbbing head.

So it is settled
Neither the honey nor the honey-bee
Is to be mine again.

I was dressed again, or was dressing, when the downstairs buzzer rang.

I buzzed back and leaned over the stairwell to see, on the railing, a hand holding a cigarette, and then, as it came to the last landing, Boychick himself, smoking his cigarette and winking at me as he came up the last few steps.

It was not a quick, sprightly, gamin-like wink, but rather solemn and studious, as if produced with great effort, as if he could not, if called upon to do so, wink with the other eye.

He came in and I closed the door.

"Hi," I said. "I'll get you an ashtray."

"Is this your apartment?" he said.

"Yes," I said.

I showed him around. It was a rather bare apartment. The studio cot I slept on was a loan from the landlady. I had a bureau, several tables, thirteen bookcases, and about a thousand books.

He had finished the cigarette and started another.

"Do you always smoke?" I said.

"You remember that package of cigarettes you gave me last night?" he said. He took it out. There were only two cigarettes left.

"I smoke even when I sleep," he said. He showed me his right hand where the index and middle fingers were yellow with nicotine stains. He had small, cherub-like fingers.

"Would you like to hear a record?" I said.

I played the *Voi che sapete*. He didn't like it much.

"I've got the record of the Café Bizarre," he said. "It's got this guy on it. He's a great comedian. He tells you all about how to put down girls. I'll bring it up and play it for you sometime."

I smiled and said, "Oh, maybe we have different tastes." (Later I was to rebuke myself for having said this.)

"I thought you weren't coming," I said.

"I wasn't going to," he said. "Then I changed my mind."

He took off his coat, a plain navy wool. I hung it in the closet. He was wearing the green corduroy pants that he had worn the night before, only now there was a tear on the left leg below the knee.

"You didn't have that tear last night," I said.

Boychick took a last drag of his cigarette. It was so short that the smoke hurt his eyes.

"No," he said. "I tore it on a piece of wire when I was crossing an empty lot."

"Was that last night?" I asked.

"Yes," he said, "just before I got home. I was so tired I just jumped into bed and slept in my clothes."

"This morning," I said, "I tore the right leg of *my* pants, the same pants I was wearing last night. I tore them on a piece of wire outside a flower shop. I was trying to get that book I promised you. I couldn't get it."

"It's all right," Boychick said, putting out his cigarette, professionally and with diligence.

I paused, and then I said, "I'm sorry. When you didn't come I bequeathed your inheritance to a towel."

I looked at Boychick to see if he knew what I meant.

He did.

"Would you like to come inside and lie down?" I said.

We got up and went into the bedroom and undressed and got into bed.

"Which side do you want?" I said.

"Either side is ok with me," he said.

I gave him the window side, a little embarrassed since, if he wanted to get out, it would be harder for him. I felt sad that I didn't trust him yet.

"I'm going to gargle," I said.

I got out of bed and went into the bathroom and poured the gargle, Odol.

"Do you want to gargle?" I called in to him.

He padded out of the bedroom and came into the bathroom and gargled with great earnestness.

I stared at his nakedness. It was the first time I had really looked at him since he had taken his clothes off. He had the pink and whiteness of a girl and that was relieved only by a huge erection that seemed an artificial addition, like that of the youth in Shakespeare's sonnet.

"Gosh," I thought. "Is he that excited over *me?*"

"She's all yours," he said, handing over the glass of garglewater and going back to bed.

I gargled quickly and followed him.

The first thing I noticed when I got under the covers was that, even though it was only a thirty-six-inch mattress, we were not crowded.

And then Boychick began to kiss me, his first kiss on my left shoulder where, cradled by the pillow, it met my neck.

Wow!

What kissing! What wonderful kissing we did! Not one single big kiss but many small ones, yet none thinking itself small, or feeling the need to register, each just coming closer to immensity, like the sun growing big and red as it reaches the horizon or flowing quickly liquid, like water from a pitcher of earthenware, coming to the parched earth at midday.

Useless, useless, I know, to attempt to capture or describe this feeling. I can only say that, to my memory, I had never felt such happiness, nor could have imagined it, nor, even now writing of it, really remember it, only perhaps equate it with the wonderful dizzy tiredness when, as a child, one runs across a field and then, lying down quickly, finds the sky overhead racing dizzily and feels the very clouds a part of oneself.

"Do you feel wonderful?" I asked Boychick.

"Yes," he said.

"I feel very wonderful," I said. "Kiss me."

We kissed.

"Let me smell your breath," I said.

He opened his mouth. He still had a child's teeth, not fully grown in yet. They looked like little tombstones, being separated still. His breath didn't smell bad. I had thought it would, with all his smoking.

"I smell something odd," I said.

"What?" Boychick said, concerned.

"I don't know," I said. I smelled his chest, armpits, hair.

"No," I said, "I guess it's not you."

"What's it smell like?" he said.

"Iron glue," I said.

"I told my mother I was going to work today," he said. "That's how I got out of the house. I have to go to work right after supper."

"Do you work?" I said.

"Five days a week," he said.

I think that he went on to mention the type of work, the place where he worked, and the hours, but I didn't listen, and then he was telling me about his father, some complaint, adding now that he wasn't his real father. "My father died before

I was born," he said. "I only knew about it last year. My mother showed me the clipping."

"What happened?" I said.

"He was in the army," Boychick said. "He was trying to steal a plane and the engine came out."

"It must have hurt," I said.

"No," he said, "he was killed instantly. The engine fell on his chest."

He went on to tell me his father's name, which was his last name, and then the name of his stepfather, the German. I wanted to write down the names, but I didn't.

I kissed him, when he finished telling about his father, feeling the odd public cheapness of my consolation, like that of someone dropping a dime in a JNF box when he leaves a delicatessen. For the loss of a father, what can a kiss do?

"There's a pool around here," I said, "would you like to go swimming?"

A moment of silence and then Boychick said, "If it's all right with you I'd just like to stay here."

This is the greatest compliment ever paid me.

We lay in each other's arms for a long time and it was as if God were swinging us in a big hammock strung across the ends of the Universe.

I pulled up the shade of the window.

"Can't they see us?" Boychick said.

"No," I said. "There's no light in this room. And even if they did, they'd just see two people in a bed. See that?" I pointed to the roof of the Manhattan Yeshiva across the way.

"At eight o'clock tonight," I said, "a pair of fire-red horses with a chariot will appear upon the room. You and I—" here I kissed him "—wrapped in a very good ermine-trimmed electric blanket, will get into the chariot, and—TO THE EAST!

"Over the Ocean! So high the biggest waves will just be small white dashes. The wind will come roaring through our hair, we'll sift through clouds and see the moon close up, biggest friendliest moon in the world!"

Boychick giggled.

"And then," I said, "we'll have crossed the ocean and come to Europe. We'll see the farmlands of Normandy, spread out like patches on a quilt—" Here I sat on top of him. Over the covers, we touched noses. "And then," I said, "down below the rooftops of Paris—" a kiss here "—green, rusted bronze, gleaming in the moonlight. . . . And cobbled streets."

Boychick grabbed me and kissed me.

"Why?" I said. "Tell my why? What is it about me that you love? Is it my big ears? My missing teeth? My chest?"

"Everything," he said, grabbing me and kissing me again.

I slipped under the covers and we circled our arms around each other and fell into an endless kiss, chest and stomach, legs and feet all moving against each other, seeming each other, seeming each to lose their own definition.

Then Boychick abruptly turned his back to me, and I knew he wanted me to get into his behind.

And then—oh Reader—how can I say it! I didn't have a hardon!

After two years of Freudian therapy and two and a half years of Horneyan analysis! Hardons every morning, every night, during the day on the subway just from rubbing against

37

someone I wouldn't spit on, hardons while at supper at the Chock Full o'Nuts, hardons while standing on the corner waiting for a bus, but now—with the most beautiful boy in the world and he with the most beautiful ass (pink and white, perfect globes like chest of heroine on cover of cheap historical novel)—*nothing!*

I reflected grimly about the possibility of a Divine Power, also wondered if this could happen in a socialist America.

My cock and balls were sweaty and swollen and the pubic hair clung around them like seaweed around a drowned body.

"Boychick," I said, "I can't make it. I guess it must be from doing it just before you got here."

"It's all right," he said, turning around and kissing me.

He stroked my stomach and abdomen and then, reaching down tentatively, as if he felt he'd be rebuked, stroked my cock.

"You don't have to," I whispered, and he quickly took his hand away.

I lifted the head of my cock and looked at it—it trying to look like the cap on a Chinese mushroom, something it had been trying to do ever since it saw Fantasia. "Stupid cock!" I said. "Never will I talk to you again! How could you do this to me? Do you see that beautiful ass over there?"

Here I turned its little fireman's cap toward Boychick. He giggled.

"The most beautiful ass in the world and/or universe!" I said. "And *this* is the way you behave!"

"It's all right," said Boychick.

"When you saw me," I said, "what did I look like?"

"You were scared," he said.

"Could you tell I was queer?" I said.

"I could tell—" he snapped his fingers "—like that."

"How do I look to you?" I said.

He closed his eyes and said, "I see you as a handsome masculine man."

I burst out laughing.

"You're saying that with your eyes closed," I said.

"What time is it?" he said.

I looked at the clock.

"It's twenty to four," I said.

"I've got to leave at four," he said. "It takes two hours to get home and I've got to eat supper and get to work."

I examined a callus on one of his short, stubby fingers.

"You wouldn't believe what that's from," he said.

"What?" I said.

"It's from work," he said.

I didn't ask him to tell me again what kind of work. Later I was to regret not asking.

We lay in each other's arms for several minutes. Winter seemed to have come in after the neutral evening of the night before. The sky had turned a rich pink, like rose petals, contrasting oddly with the green painted railings of the Yeshiva as if to reproduce the colors from some actual rosebush, the green of the bush, the red of the rose. I glanced at the clock. It was five minutes to four.

"We have five more minutes," I said. "Do you want me to jack you off?"

"If you want to," he said.

39

I looked down at his cock, which, uncircumcised, looked like a large earthworm.

"Were you born in New York City?" I said.

"Yes," he said.

"Then how come you weren't circumcised?" I said.

"I was born in Akron, Ohio," he said. And then added, "My mother was married five times"—this with great indignation, as if she should not have married so many times.

He was jacking himself off and I went to get some toilet paper for him to wipe himself with.

When I came back I asked, "Do you jack off often?"

He looked disturbed and then said, "No, only about two or three times a week."

I had the feeling then, which was often to return later, that everything he did and said was tentative, and, in his confusion as to what to say to make a good impression, the final speech had an amoebic pseudopod motion.

He came and wiped himself off and I lay beside him.

I looked out the window at the red sky and wished that four o'clock would never come.

It had passed.

"Come," I said. "We'll take a shower."

When he had finished dressing, he asked for some hair tonic and started to comb his hair.

"Do you want the hair tonic?" I asked. "I don't use it. I got it as a free dividend."

"All right," he said. "Can you wrap it for me in a paper bag?"

"Yes," I said, but my voice took on a harsh, mechanical quality, for it came over me with sudden bitterness that perhaps I was being taken advantage of. I cannot give a rationale for this now.

Even as I write this, I want to insert in the story any further conversation to keep away the moment when the door has to open and we leave.

But it has to come.

"Ready?" I said.

"Yup."

He put on his coat and lit his cigarette.

I stood with him beside the door and then we kissed. He lifted his chin so that I wouldn't upset his combed hair.


I persuaded him to use the IRT to get home and we began to walk toward the station.

It was always to be, when I was with him, that I was very manic. I felt terribly young. Boychick, on the other hand, always seemed older than he was and very dignified. So, when we were hurrying to the 96th Street station, it was I who kept running ahead.

It is of interest to me, having marked this behavior in others, that, although we wish very much to please those we love, our faults seem to have lives of their very own, flourishing astoundingly in the presence of the Beloved, as if this presence provided, not the means of cutting these faults short, but an environment congenial to their growth.

Thus I, who have the faults of over-levity, childishness and effeminacy, found myself accentuating them with Boychick—who obviously disliked them—and seeming unconscious of his reaction. I was jumping in the air, perhaps in reality.

"When we get to the station," I said, "there's a bookstore

a block or so away. I'll try to get you that *Tristan and Iseult*."

"I'm broke," the boy said. "I won't get paid until next Thursday."

I wondered when he had been paid last that he had used up a week's pay by Friday, but I didn't say anything. I had cashed my father's check and I had a ten dollar bill.

"Are you sure you're taking me to the station?" he said.

"Yes," I said, "and it's an express. I'm on your side, remember?"

He laughed.

From the corner of 96th and Broadway we walked two more blocks to the paperback book store.

"I'm going to be late and get fired," Boychick said. "F-i-r-e-d."

"I'll be quick," I said.

"I'll wait outside," he said.

I wondered again why he always wanted to wait outside the shop. Did he feel I looked so much like a fairy that I would give the game away?

This thought upsetting me, I got the book and exchanged a few words with the man at the cash register. The book cost a little less than a dollar, and I wondered if the Boychick would think that I had bought it for him because it was cheaper than the Gottfried von Strassburg version.

I looked at the cover. It was an ugly green, although the picture of Tristan and Iseult had a slight charm. Somehow I hoped that something in the story would ring a bell for him, remind him of me.

He was waiting outside.

"Could I have some change for carfare?" he said.

I gave him a dollar with the book. He opened the book and looked at the page.

"It's got big print," he said. "Thanks."

I wondered if he were being ironic, thinking I was giving him a "baby" book, but if this was the case I could not detect his irony.

I left him, as I had left him the evening before, at the top of the subway stairs.

I STOOD on the street corner staring (one has to stare at something) at the magazines laid out on the news stand counter. Foreign language newspapers, also magazines, little film reviews, socialist publications and—right beside them—muscle magazines with pictures of men in jockstraps.

Interesting, I thought. I guess if you get the muscle magazines often enough you even become interested in weight-lifting.

I walked past four shoeshine boys, all of whom said shine, Mister, although they could see I was wearing tennis sneakers that were falling to pieces.

Why had I let him go into the false, treacherous subway, slip so into dirt and indifference? Would he get to his job on time, would he be fired, and more important—most important—would I ever know?

Just at the moment we had crossed Broadway at 96th Street I had said to him, "My phone's disconnected. I hope to have it connected by the middle of next month. If you want to call me, please do, and we can get together."

"Sure," Boychick had said.

There was something else Boychick had said.

When we had been in bed talking about his fights with his stepfather (who, it seemed, never allowed anything but Strauss waltzes to be played on the phonograph), Boychick had smiled and said, "And it's so wonderful, everyone else loving you."

"Good lord!" I had said (rushing in, like a scholar, to prevent the misuse of a term). "Do you think that I love you?"

Boychick's face had fallen.

"Don't you?" he had said.

What had happened then? I guess I had kissed him, gently, to keep from further discussion of the matter.

Now, walking home on this November evening, I realized that I was in love.

When I came back to the apartment I went into the living room. I had cleared the long table—one of those door tables with black cast iron legs—with the intention of studying my Old English grammar.

It had always been my theory that sex would disturb study but now I found that this was not the case.

I seemed to be seeing more clearly than I had ever seen before, and found myself more willing to learn the verbs.

Even learning verb forms, itself an echo of my high school days with French and Spanish, gave me a sense of being like Boychick. I even thought what fun it would be to have Boychick learn the Old English verb forms.

The downstairs buzzer rang and I answered—I always answer the buzzer—and then I leaned over the curving stairwell and heard the ascending footsteps.

I know this is not true but it would almost seem to be—
that the footsteps of the welcome visitor are altogether different from those of the unwelcome. These were the footsteps of the unwelcome visitor.

The Unwelcome Visitor is not simply a person who is
visiting us and is—at that time and/or place—unwelcome.
The unwelcomeness comes long before the visit. I suspect that
it is such a vital part of the person that, at some future date
when the chromosomal makeup is more thoroughly known,
we will locate the particular chromosome that has the unwelcome gene.

But let us allow the Unwelcome Visitor to enter since,
in the time that it has taken the reader to peruse these few
words, the Unwelcome Visitor has ascended the steps, the
rate of ascent being exactly the same as that of the Welcome
Visitor, or perhaps—indeed, invariably faster.

"Oh," I said, "Norman."

"Yes," he said. "Norman. Were you expecting someone
else?"

This, the first question the Unwelcome asks, is as invariable
as the question of the Bad Son at Passover Seder.

"Is anybody here?"

Please note, Reader, that it is not due to condensation of
dialogue for the purposes of fiction that I have not included
any sentence such as "Am I disturbing you?" or even "I
hope I'm not disturbing you." The Unwelcome Visitor, due
to the nature of his function, cannot utter either of these
sentences.

"No," I said. "No one's here."

"Oh," he said. "That's good. I wanted to talk to you."

He sat down in the sling chair and pressed his fingers on the bridge of his nose and said, "I've been doing a lot of thinking."

A moment of silence after this.

He looked like the overworked, impotent husband in an old Elisabeth Bergner movie.

"Could you get me something to drink?" he said.

"I've got milk and orange juice," I said. "I can make coffee but I've only got instant."

Norman raised one of his bony hands in a gesture duplicating that of Gandhi as he forgave his assassin.

"No," he said. "I'll just have the orange juice. About a six-ounce glass. And put an extra teaspoon of sugar in it. I need the energy. Do you have confectioner's sugar?"

"No," I said.

"It's all right," he said. "You can use regular sugar. I'll try to organize myself while you're getting it."

When I came back with the juice I said, "Norman, I don't want to rush you, but I have to leave in about fifteen minutes."

Norman closed his eyes and leaned his head back. Since the sling chair had a low back, there was a sudden startling view of his thin bony neck, the protruding Adam's apple, giving him the appearance of having at one time been hanged.

"Poor Leo," he said, "he can't even take a few minutes to listen to an old friend."

"Perhaps it would help you to write down your thoughts," I said. "Then I would be able to consider any questions you put to me at leisure and give some time to my answer."

"No," he said. "You know I can't write. I still have my block. No. I've got to work things out verbally."

47

He put his bony head forward and rested his forehead in one of his bony hands, this in silence to show me he was organizing his valuable words for my benefit.

If I could have tossed him out the window I would have.

"What would you say," Norman said, "if I told you that I was thinking of going back to school?"

I couldn't have cared less if he'd crawled into his own little asshole and disappeared forever.

"It sounds like a good idea," I said, looking at the clock. I would get up in five minutes and put on my coat.

"I've been away for ten years," he said. "Ten years. Think of that." This as if he was Buck Rogers returning to Earth, viewing same from panoramic window of spaceship.

"Do you think I can make it?" he said. "It won't be easy. I'm not kidding myself."

"I'm sure you will," I said.

"How are you doing?" he said in his I'm-Gerontion-let-me-feel-your-balls voice.

"All right," I said.

"What are you studying?" he said. Two old friends having a conversation about our mutual affairs.

"Old English," I said.

"Is that your period?" he said.

"You don't take a period at NYU when you go for your master's," I said.

Norman shook his little coconut head.

"You shouldn't let them do that to you," he said. "You should try to make a period."

"I'm concentrating on early English literature," I said.

48

"Let me see that book," he said. He waved one of his bony fingers at my Old English grammar.

I handed it to him.

He turned its pages and nodded his head and then handed it back to me.

"Any good?" he said, in his wonderful T. S. Eliot tired voice.

"Yes," I said.

"How much German do you know?" he said.

"None," I said.

"And you're trying to learn Old English without a basic foundation in German? It *is* German."

"German is not a prerequisite for the course," I said.

"They're fools," he said, wiping the spittle from his chin. "The whole pack at NYU are a bunch of shovels."

"They are excellent scholars," I said. "All my teachers are excellent."

Norman rubbed the tired bridge of his nose again. "I was thinking of the history department. I'm thinking of going into history. The history department at NYU is shit. If I can't get into Columbia I won't go anywhere."

"I hope you get into Columbia," I said, wanting to open the window and send him flying over Morningside Park and the Cathedral of St. John the Divine.

He felt the lumps on his forehead. "I'm thinking of going into the ninth century," he said. "Alcuin."

Alcuin was eighth century, but I did not interrupt, knowing that this would only lead to more words.

"I have a feeling of kinship with them," he said (here a

49

wave of his skeleton hand in the air). "There is a feeling of greyness to the world, a searching. You know what I mean?"

"Yes," I said. "It sounds like a good idea."

"I need to write a thesis," he said, covering his eyes like an actor in a Greek tragedy at the moment of Revelation. "It's not something just for the teachers. I need it for myself. I want to write something for publication, to prove to myself that I can write."

"I hope you get into Columbia," I said. With the repetition of this sentence came again the image of Norman flying out the window.

I got up and put on my coat.

"I'm sorry we can't talk it out at greater length," I said.

Norman put on his authentic English tweed coat. "I've got to externalize," he said. "That's the only way I can get at my problems."

I looked at Norman as we walked down Central Park West. His badness was complete in itself, like a Japanese trick box: shameless, endless, continuous egotism. Everything in the world attached to his back like a bauble. Friendship, history, marriage, apartment, even his little girlchild, all appendages of Norman's egoism.

I thought of Boychick, of his young, beautiful body, its smell like that of fresh apples, and I wondered if I would be able to tell Norman about him. But no. For Norman with the wedding, the apartment, the wife, the child, it would only make for another verbal attack. "Leo's a fairy," this the central sentence to be stuck, like an ostrich feather, at various points on his cluttered hermit crab shell of egoism. So: "Well, Leo, are you still seeing that kid? What do you

50

do with him?" or again, "Well, how's my favorite cock-sucker?" This last to stick in my shoulder with the professional flair of a bullfighter.

What a wretched, dry, colorless world he lived in.

Hardly hearing Norman's interesting-effective-theoretical-allusive conversation, I only wondered why I had tolerated it for so many years—these worse-than-useless fake words that seemed to have been brought forth only to distract me from an appointment I would have to keep.

Here one sings:

Who is Norman, what is he?
That I should let him bore me?


"Come on up," said Norman. (Let the reader note that the sentence is not "Why don't you come on up?" or "Would you like to come up?"). "Sylvia's expecting you. I told her that I'd bring you over for supper."

"I'd love to," I said, "but I have to make a phone call."

"Make it in our house," said Norman. (Note the imperative form of the verb.)

"No, thank you," I said. "It's a private telephone call."

"All right," he said, and released me.

T HE IDEA of a devil or a Satan seems primitive but, as T.H. Gaster had tried to explain in his lectures on the background of the New Testament, it was an essential part of the vocabulary of the Near East. To the Hebrew mind, when something happened, it was caused to happen.

So, if one struck a match, it ignited, not because the combination of elements in the matchhead had been oxidized, but because an agent, an angel so to speak—one single angel with one single mission—had accomplished that mission, had lit the match. For each lighted match there had been or would be an angel.

Let us then take the case of the match that does not light. What are we to make of that?

That is where Satan enters. It is the function of the Devil to prevent things from happening. Indeed, such is the connotation of the name Satan, which means "the interferer." It is, then, a devil who prevents the match from being lighted, standing in the way of the angel who would light it.

So now I regarded Norman, and his world, each word

and motion, each invitation and gesture, as designed only to prevent things from happening.

So, it even seemed to me, he had come to fill some vital part of my day, to prevent some action from leading to fruition. Norman's entire life was designed to prevent the Asking of the Great Question, for once asked it might even be answered. His was the task of infinite postponement.

I had walked along West 96th Street to the corner of Broadway, that same corner where only a few hours ago, I had left Boychick. Now, standing near the subway entrance, I could almost hear his voice again: "I'm going to lose my job. Jay, oh, be, job."

Would he lose it and would I ever know?

After leaving the constricting presence of Norman, I had realized for the first time how alive I felt. I had never felt so good. How was this possible? You lie in bed with someone, rub against him a little, kiss him and then—feel so alive? How does it work? Would it work again?

I had not lied to Norman when I said that I was going to make a telephone call. I was calling Ariela.

I guess Ariela is my best friend in the city.

Ariela is red-headed, in her forties. Her father died when she was in her twenties and she has an independent income. She has traveled in France, Austria, Crete, Greece, even Russia (she at that time a Red). She was—is—kind, intelligent and—most important—she is very fond of me.

I called her from a phone in the pharmacy on the corner and told her about Boychick. "And I feel so *good*. What am I going to do?"

"I guess you're going to go to bed with him as long as you like it," she said.

"But I'm so afraid of getting into trouble," I said. "He's a minor. He's only sixteen."

"Well," said Ariela, "you know heterosexuals have troubles, too." We have to contend with the possibility of pregnancy, disease, but one can't think of all these things. I never did. When are you going to see him again?"

"I didn't make a meet with him. I just told him that my phone would be connected in the middle of next month and that he could call me up if he wanted to."

"Do you have his telephone number?" said Ariela.

"No," I said.

"Well," said Ariela, "that's not very smart. If you wanted to see him again so much, how is it that you didn't make an appointment with him?"

"I didn't realize," I said, "when I was saying goodby to him that I would want to see him again. I didn't want to commit myself."

"What's his name?" said Ariela.

"I can't remember," I said.

"Well," said Ariela, "you couldn't have been very interested in him if you didn't pay any attention to his name. Didn't you listen to him when he talked?"

"I thought I did," I said.

"No one ever listens," said Ariela.

"He said he swims at the St. George all the time," I said. "Do you think if I keep on going to that pool he'll show up there?"

"I guess so," said Ariela, "if you go often enough."

"Oh, Ariela!" I said. "I want to see him so much!"

"If you want to enough," said Ariela, "you will."

I thanked her for her advice and hung up. I see Ariela almost every Wednesday night at the English Folk Country Dance Society. After the dancing session we go for toasted muffins and coffee at the Twin Brothers Restaurant. That is, I drink coffee. She has hot milk.

She lives two blocks from the St. George Hotel.

The callus he had on his hand from working, what kind of work? Where did he work? Where did he live?

Somewhere in Brooklyn, at this moment, he was working. He would go home after work. His room had a double decker bed. His father played Strauss waltzes, his sister was a lesbian who played Ahmad Jamal records on a hi-fi set, drank Thunderbirds, had an Orthodox Jewish Puerto Rican girl as roommate, went to the Café Bizarre. And he often went swimming at the St. George.

ST. GEORGE," said Dr. Freedman, "is of course the Redcrosse Knight, although modified for Spenser's specific purposes."

She turned and smiled at me. She looked quite insane.

We had come to the major part of Dr. Freedman's Sidney and Spenser course, the study of Spenser's *Faerie Queene*. We were now discussing Book I and would go on, each Friday night, to discuss another book.

Dr. Freedman looked at me again.

"St. George, like the other knights, is sent by Gloriana from the Land of Faeries."

I was seated on Dr. Freedman's right. It was a colloquim and we sat at a table. The three non-paying, auditing students were on seats placed against the wall near the door. One of them, an Irish-looking boy, smiled at me and adjusted his crotch.

"Oh God," I thought. "The subtle type. Probably reads Jane Austen and Henry James."

I smiled at him and winked.

"Una represents, of course, pure wisdom. Spenser expected his readers to know this." Dr. Freedman turned and gave me a wicked smile. "The fact that the Redcrosse Knight could possibly be deceived by the false Una indicates that he does not yet completely apprehend the nature of Truth."

One of the girls raised her hand.

"I found the ordeal of the Redcrosse Knight in the House of Holiness very distasteful," she said.

Dr. Freedman made a face.

"Spenser didn't like it either," she said. "He does not dwell on the physical tortures at length." She patted her copy of the book. "Spenser simply feels that repentance must entail a certain amount of suffering and he makes that plain. That's all. It has to be there," and she patted the book again several times. "Will someone try to keep the windows open at least a little?" she said. "I'm sorry that those near the windows will have to suffer." She smiled at the use of the word "suffering" in connection with the classroom. "But it appears that if we sin by smoking—as I do myself—some of us at least will have to pay by wearing our coats during class. I assume that if any of you are prone to stiff necks or catching colds, you will be able to get other seats, away from the windows. I want to say that I am very pleased with the class recitations and, since this seems like a good method, I think we'll stick to it. Next week, if you can, I would like you all to prepare in advance a five-minute paper on the subject of the Bower of Bliss, the twelfth canto of the second book."

She looked at her watch. The Irish boy was already taking his coat off the hook. A real commuter.

"I guess we'll have to stop now," said Dr. Freedman, giving us a bittersweet, goodnight smile.

The Irish commuter had left.

I picked up my coat and decided to go to the men's room before I got into the subway. I was going to Brooklyn, to the St. George pool.

As I went into the men's room, the Irish commuter left, glancing at me briefly and nodding his head.

$B$OYCHICK was not at the pool. This did not disturb me, for in that story I seem already to have begun to write he could not be at the pool the first time I looked for him there.

But there was another fiction-motif that came to me, this one less comforting. It was the theme of disaster through chance. In my childhood there had been any number of movies that had stressed the coincidence theme—a soldier, for instance, in love with a girl and then having amnesia. Somehow, before the end of the film, the boy and girl would get together—he would be knocked on the head again and recover his memory. But the thought that some slight physical accident, a knock on the head, a letter not addressed properly, an appointment missed, could result in permanent separation from the loved one—this thought was a sharp barb.

I have two great disabilities. A bad memory and near-sightedness. Since I would not be wearing my glasses at the pool, was there not the chance that, on the day he was there, I would not see him, might not, with my bad memory, recognize him?

But that night, looking around, I could easily see that he was not there. It was a cold night and there were few people at the pool, just several couples watching television at the poolside. They were almost all Catholics, this evidenced by the miraculous medals worn around their necks.

On this first night I set up the routine that I was to use for each visit thereafter. I would do ten widths of the pool (about one hundred and fifty yards), then go to the steam room and sit there for the count of one hundred breaths, then go and lie under the sun lamps for the count of one hundred breaths, then back to the pool for another ten widths. I would swim in the pool three times each evening, which made about four hundred and fifty yards. The swimming pool-steam room-sunbath cycle repeated three times took less than an hour. This was the time I planned to spend each day at the pool. I would go at a different time each day, hoping to hit upon the time and place when Boychick would be there.

On the way home that evening I stopped at the Café Bizarre.

I saw a pile of records near the entrance as I went in and could almost hear Boychick's voice saying, "This guy has a wonderful record. It tells all about how to put down girls."

And I, so stupid, had wanted to be superior. I had smiled and said, "Our tastes are not the same." How gladly I would have accepted the record if he had come with it! How far indeed Hymettus, the bees upon it—lost now the honey, the honey bee, the hills and clover.

The Café Bizarre was very crowded that Friday night.

Some sort of show was going on in the front. I paid the dollar entrance fee and found a seat at a long table with six other people. In front of me were two blond young boys wearing serge suits of different shades of blue. They looked stiff with embarrassment, as I had looked the first time I went to a nightclub.

On the stage a young girl was playing the guitar very badly. She was also singing. Was she singing as badly as she was playing? It was only after she had been singing for some time that I realized the song was on an Oranim Zabar record, "*Va Yevan*"—"And he built."

Moreover Uzziah built towers in Jerusalem . . .
And fortified them
And built towers in the desert
and dug many wells . . .

Chronicles II 26:9-10

But the girl was singing Eliahu (Elijah) instead of Uziahu (Uzziah). Was it possible that she felt the prophet had done the work instead of the king? Of course not. She had listened to the song on the record of the Oranim Zabar troupe and was now repeating it badly. There was no excuse for it. The lyrics were available in Hebrew, even with convenient transliteration into Roman letters in the booklet that came with the record.

The two boys, looking very sad, stared at the stage.

The waitress came over with two frappes. "Are you the two with the Voodoo Surprise?" she said.

"Yes," one of the boys said.

"She set down the frappes, spilling syrup from both on the table.

"Ooops," she said. "I'll get a sponge."

She announced the sponge as if it were the next act in a circus.

A small line of couples waiting for free tables had formed on one side. They were *all* couples, very young and very well-dressed, the boys wearing jackets and overcoats. What was I wearing? Either my short jacket (made of grey canvas, with black elastic at the waist and cuffs), or my winter coat of grey twill with a mouton collar. This winter coat had been very good but now it was old and worn and no amount of dry cleaning could ever keep it from looking dirty.

The waitress came back, not with a sponge but with several napkins which she placed over the spilled syrup. She left them there. "Is there anything else?"

"I think the Voodoo Surprise is only seventy-five cents," said the older boy. "You have eighty-five down here."

"I'd like a glass of water," said the younger boy.

"We're out of ice," said the waitress.

"I'll have it without ice," the younger boy said.

"Did you get your order yet?" the waitress asked me.

"I haven't ordered yet," I said.

"I'm sorry," she said, "this isn't my usual table. Would you like a Voodoo Surprise?"

"No," I said, "just a hot chocolate."

"There's a minimum of seventy-five cents," she said.

"Just a hot chocolate," I said.

Up front a man was singing "Aupres de ma blonde," accompanied by the girl who had been singing about Elijah. She now contented herself with striking the same chord on a guitar every few seconds. Some weak applause followed the completion of this number, and then, passing along the line of waiting couples, came a man who was, undoubtedly, the next performer. He was wearing a fishnet over his chest and there was an imitation leopard skin draped over that. I, determined not to hear him, had put on my glasses and was looking to see if Boychick, with or without his sister, was around.

He was not there.

Dark and crowded as the place was, I would have spotted him. His hair alone would have been sufficiently conspicuous. All the males there had hair much darker than his (excepting the two serge-suited blond boys opposite me), and all of them—almost without exception—had very short haircuts. I remembered Boychick's elaborate haircomb, the breaking wave over his forehead.

I was half-minded to leave before the hot chocolate arrived, but it came just as the fishnet Negro gained the stage.

It was the worst hot chocolate I have ever had. The powder was still in clumps in the liquid and there was even chocolate powder on the saucer.

The waitress had settled it down on the table, spilling some, announcing, it seemed to me, almost before she had spilled it, "I'll get napkins."

"Waitress," said the older boy.

"We're out of whipped cream right now," she explained to me. "It's Friday night. If you want to ask me later, I might try to get you some."

"Waitress," said the older boy.

"Do you want another Voodoo Surprise?" she asked.

"You haven't changed our checks," the boy said.

"You pay when you go out," the waitress said. "You just leave a tip."

"No," the boy said. "The Voodoo Surprise is only seventy-five cents."

She took the bills and changed the sum, crossing out the eighty-five cents.

"I don't have an eraser," she said, "but I put my initials down. If they stop you at the door tell them I didn't have an eraser."

"May I have a check?" I said.

"I've used up all mine," she said. "Wait, I'll get another." She went away.

On the stage, the man in the fishnet had begun. "Hey you—" he said, "*you*, not you! That young girl there. No use stroking that chin of yours. Won't grow you no beard."

The waitress came back and placed a check for two dollars and some cents next to my hot chocolate puddle. Then she looked at me again and quickly took it away.

"That wasn't your bill," she said. "You're the hot chocolate."

"That's me," I said, "the hot chocolate."

Up front, the fishnet Negro had been interrupted by the Elijah guitarist.

"Wait a second, Frank," she said, her voice carrying into the microphone. "PEOPLE! I know that you've been enjoying this show, and this is your opportunity to show your appreciation. The artists who come here work without pay.

They come to share with you their enjoyment of music. I know that you want to thank them and show your appreciation. So, please, in a little while a girl will come around with a basket. Please put what you can into it, as much as you can. Please remember that these artists are not being paid. Whatever you give will be much appreciated. Thank you. Frank."

I picked up my new check for eighty-five cents, a sum I was not going to dispute, and, leaving a tip, got up to go to the exit.

Before I could get away from the table the girl-with-the-basket appeared. It was tied to a pole like a church collection basket and already had several dollars in it. The two blue-serge boys gave a dollar each, and the basket stopped in front of me. I shook my head. The basket made another circuit of the table and stopped again in front of me.

I looked at the girl. She looked exactly like the girl who had been singing the Elijah song on stage. Long black hair, unbound, a black turtleneck sweater, and black tights. She had set her mouth very firmly. I shook my head again and left, thinking how odd it was that these bad performances had come to mean "art" for the girl. How could she be so mistaken? Couldn't she even compare these "artists" with those she had heard on records, or on the radio? Or was it that she felt that the artists of the Café Bizarre were, in some way, the true, uncommercial artists, the others being slick, having sold out? Where had she come from, that the Café Bizarre was her haven, location of all meaning, worthy of all allegiance? I imagined a home in the Bronx, Jewish, her parents both working, herself most alive in the nexus whose center was the argument that preceded her departure for the Village and followed her return.

The argument on Departure:

"Are you going out like this?"

Response: "What do you think?"

"Do you think I'm going to let you go out in the street like this?"

Response: "You can't stop me."

"Do you ever think what the neighbors are thinking of you?"

Response: "I never *think* about the neighbors, and if I *did*, I wouldn't *care* what they thought."

"Do you care what your parents think? Do you care about your own mother and father?"

Response: (None)

"Would you like to hear what we think?"

Response: "Mother, if I don't leave right now I'm going to be late for work."

A moment of silence, then:

"Are you going to work dressed like that? Does the boss see you dressed like this?"

Response: "Mama, all the girls dress like this."

A moment of silence, then:

"So, if all the girls dress like that does that mean that you have to dress like that? Tell me something. Suppose all the girls were whores—"

Response: "MAMA! If you say that word again in my presence, so help me God I'm going to move out of the house. And I'm going to tell Papa what you called me. Don't wait up for me and don't expect me to tell you where I've been. I'm growing up, Mom, and you just won't accept the fact."

And so she faced me there with the same determination with which she had closed the door of the apartment in the Bronx. The others at the table with their bourgeois dress had somehow paid their allegiance to her black tights and turtleneck sweater. It was only I, dressed so shabbily, who had withheld, and so she defiantly held the tray in front of me, as proud as any Christian, bitter as any member of the Maquis, begger-proud as Genet (whose *Thieves' Journal* she had not read, but whose name would set her nodding eagerly).

Leaving the cafe I passed the long line of couples waiting to get in, and then I realized that Boychick and his sister and her friends would not be at the Bizarre on weekends. Weekend nights were for tourists. I remembered now that Boychick had *said* that he would be going to a party given by his sister. If he were in the Village he would be at his sister's room.

When I was younger, much younger—during World War II—my brother and I had played a game called Submarine. There was a gird, a series of squares made by criss-crossing ten lines down a sheet of paper with ten lines across, and each player had his own sheet of one hundred squares. The vertical squares were labeled A through J, the horizontal one to ten. Then each filled in the squares with letters spelling "submarine," "destroyer," "cruiser," or "convoy." You could write each word horizontally, or vertically, but continuously—one letter per square. The game would consist of naming a square, say G5, and then, if that square on your opponent's sheet contained a letter from submarine, or destroyer, or cruiser, or convoy, he would have to tell you which letter. A "hit" allowed you another chance immediately, but if you missed, the next turn of course went to your opponent.

I was playing Submarine. I would be, at some time, in the Café Bizarre, or walking in the Village, or at the St. George—in the swimming pool, shower, steam room—and, if I were lucky, one day Boychick would be there.

It never occurred to me, during any of my plans, that the simple conjunction of our bodies in the same square would not be sufficient. My only torment was the thought that I might by some mean accident or oversight allow my prey to slip through my fingers. The thought that he might be here, even now, occurred to me as I raised my eyes to the windows along West 4th Street, the thought falling through me like a meteorite hitting with impossible speed a body in outer space.

There was, in this game of Submarine, a word I wanted to put on my chart: TELEPHONE. I had told him that he could telephone. I was determined that he would be able to. That night I wrote to my friend Adam, asking him for the money to pay my back telephone bill.

LIKE ARIELA, Adam is not essential to this story and can be skipped by those who, having a mechanistic theory of existence, cannot believe in true friendship. (Of course these same people cannot believe in love and will, therefore, never understand this story at all. But since they have never understood anything, they will not see their non-comprehension as a hiatus of any sort. There will only be a continuation of the greyness of their existence.)

Adam was my friend, my best and most beloved friend, closer to me than my brother.

We had been roommates in Columbia when he was a sophomore and a junior. He came from a suburb of Chicago, had a round red face and red hair, and was altogether placid and loving.

I had loved him in college and when he was in the navy serving in Japan and when he was in Harvard getting his master's. I had loved him when he was in Paris at the Sorbonne. We had never been lovers, after the flesh as they say, although I had made every possible endeavor in that direction. Adam was, to use the scientific terminology, exclusively heterosexual.

What is it like—this desire to love someone, or rather this act of loving, for, though I never had what Kinsey could describe as intercourse with Adam, yet I was, for many years, very much his lover. Plato described it in his *Symposium* and *Phaedrus* all too well. It is the desire for, the reaching toward, the possession of, the good.

When one loves someone, a curious pride is born in the lover. He feels—why I cannot tell—that the various excellencies possessed by the Beloved are, by some extension, possessed by himself. Not indeed that I, loving Adam, could then exercise his virtues, but that I, in adoring him, adored these virtues, and so supported them, their life, in him. It was—I hope I am not being sacrilegious—as if I were, like God, the creator of these virtues, or at least their sustainer, because I adored them.

And so, as with a planet whose path cannot be explained without reference to some larger body, far removed and often out of sight of the viewer, so the reader may not understand my future actions, unless he takes account of my friends, Ariela and Adam. How often I had taken refuge in both the red-haired Ariela and the red-haired Adam. So real were their feelings to me that often, when complaining to them, or exhibiting some grief, I am overcome with shame at the pettiness of my complaint, feeling it too small an injury to cause their discomfort.

And it has often been my conviction that, although I might never be able to repay the debt I owe these friends, yet it might be possible at some later time in my life to befriend someone else as I had been befriended by them.

Secrets.

How often, when a child, I had felt full of secrets and the necessity of keeping them.

How now, sitting here, I feel that the only secret I wish to know is the secret of a self that is gone.

Why do I now feel the Leo of that time so valuable? Perhaps because, like the camera in a Hitchcock thriller, he contained a valuable picture.

The picture of the classic Boychick. The secret of the classic, which secret is only hinted at in the Venus de Milo, only stated in the Parthenon, but given to us when we fall in love.

So Boychick had moved unseen through his home and classes, had paid his fare unnoticed on the bus, passed unseen through the world, until he came before me. And then he had become classic. Forever now would his narrow chest be pressed to mine, his cheeks be smooth, his eyes clear. And all these facts about him—like the tears of joy that Pascal felt and noted on a scrap of paper later sewn into the lining of his coat—so now all these words, like the revelation of the mystic, can only, to the reader, be either incomprehensible and tiresome, or, most probably, moronic, childlike.

Childlike indeed—with that hectic insistence adults find so hard to comprehend—I wanted Boychick.

THAT SATURDAY EVENING (had I studied that day? I think so), I was at the St. George again, and this time, although still no Boychick, there was, as if to demonstrate to me the excellence of my choice, a host of Boychick-like creatures, all Catholic and blond, but mindless, soul-less, sexless.

Looking at their eyes, I remembered Boychick's first glance at me, that peculiar watchfulness, like a woodland creature possessed of all the instincts for survival. And how stupid, how utterly stupid these no-sex creatures were, intent only on screaming and pushing one another into the water.

What worlds were there worth conquering for him?

What did he want? And more than that—what was there that I could give him?

Swimming in the pool with its blue-green water and blue and green mosaic tiles, I thought not of the grottoes of Italy but of the mists of Cornwall. Why this was so, I cannot tell. Perhaps because, as a careful gardener, I would want to return Boychick to some climate like that from which his stock had come.

As I swam to and fro in the pool doing my widths, each width fifteen strokes, I could almost feel the sea surging around me, the thick fog, could almost reach out and grab the rope that would haul me into the boat.

"Have we long to go?" Boychick said.

"No, lad," I said. "Ye must not worry. I've guided this craft through the Scillies a thousand times."

"What's that noise?" Boychick said.

"Only the sirens singing," I said.

"For us?" said Boychick.

"No," I said, reaching the pool's edge and pushing off again with my feet, "for Billy Graham."

It was 9:30 and this was my last lap. I climbed out, weary from answering so many of Boychick's questions. That I had not seen him did not bother me.

I dressed and took the subway uptown to the Village and walked to Jim Aiken's, an all-night diner at the corner of Sheridan Square. Boychick was not there.

I continued to walk along 4th Street till I came to Frisco's.

I never saw a gay bar that was well lighted. They always have the misty atmosphere of an aquarium whose water needs changing, and I always expect to see exhausted seaweed floating in the air and snails crawling up the mirror behind the bar.

A song by Frank Sinatra, "Nice 'n' Easy," was on the phonograph.

What is the crowd like in a gay bar? First, there are almost no women there. The men are almost all young. They are rarely effeminate in appearance although often in passing you notice effeminate mannerisms, a voice raised too high, too arch. Hands flick cigarettes with a gesture that seems more a caricature of homosexuality than a symptom.

It may be my imagination, but there does seem to be a homosexual type, perhaps simply a fashion to which various homosexuals somehow manage to conform. It consists of a certain physical appearance, a thinness and a certain odd blankness around the eyes that I have never found anything less than frightening. I imagine that if I could take the inhabitants of this bar, now about fifty or more, and sort them out, there would be only five or so that would conform to this pattern, but many more of them to some part of it. The skin smooth, the hair blond, combed back, the cigarette king-size, seeming in length and leanness like the person. The eyebrows seem slightly raised as if in permanent surprise, and then—most prominent of all—that odd blankness of the eyes.

What else? Dress. Almost always in some way eccentric. Rarely, as in my case, shabby or dirty. Gay boys almost always dress well, although they often wear too little. Even now, in this cold December, some had only short leather jackets on and—most frequent—tight blue pants. What color blue? It used to be the dark blue of work levis. Now it's a light blue, faded.

Another note: almost half the boys in the bar were Negroes.

I went to the back after getting a beer and stood there drinking it.

After a while one of the stools near the wall was vacated and I sat down.

A couple was seated at a table on my right, a fat girl and a boy. He winked at me. I winked back, lifting my eyes toward the ceiling. I am very fond of doing that.

The girl turned around.

"Would you care to join us?" she said.

My stomach sank at the sound of her voice. It was a particularly vulgar, Brooklyn woman's voice that I have always associated with meanness, cruelty, stupidity. The voice of a carnivorous creature.

I joined them.

Why, if I felt as I did, did I accept her offer? Because that's the sort of person I am: I felt ashamed I hated her so.

"What your *name?*" she said, in her dreadful voice that grated like a sandy paper coated with syrup and granulated sugar.

"Leo," I said.

"My name's *Florence!*" she said, as if she had just pulled a rabbit out of her ear, "and this is Frank! Frank's my sweetheart. We're going to be *married.*"

With this remark the two looked at each other and burst out laughing.

"We're just joking," she said. "We're cousins. Would you know, just looking at us, that we're cousins?"

"No," I said.

"You haven't really looked at us. Look. First I'm going to give you a full face and then a profile, and then I want you to look at Frank full face and profile."

The heads turned.

"There is a slight resemblance," I said.

"Someone last week said we looked like brother and sister!" she said. "And I said, 'Frank, let's get married!' "

Here she and Frank burst out laughing.

I had just bought a second beer and hastily took several swallows.

"Do you like beer?" she said.

"Yes," I said.

"I never drink beer," she said. "It's bad for my figure."

I looked at her to see if she was joking. She was almost shapelessly fat.

"Frank thinks you're *cute*," she said.

"Frank's cute, too," I said.

Florence laughed and laughed.

"Oh," she said. "Frank, did you hear what he said? He said you were cute!"

Frank smiled at me. His appearance was in no way similar to the composit image of the gay boy that I have presented. He looked, like me, Mediterranean: olive skin, dark eyes—except that, while my eyes pop out in a manner suggestive of exothalmic goiter, he squinted.

His squint—Ricky Nelson variety—gave him a shifty look, like a kitten that has drunk something alcoholic. (Please don't ask me when I've ever seen a kitten that has drunk something alcoholic.)

"Are you *gay?*" asked Florence.

"Of course not," I said. "Straightest boy in the world."

"Oh, that's *funny!*" she said. "I bet if a girl kissed you you'd drop dead."

"Haven't dropped yet," I said.

She kissed my cheek.

"I'm dead," I said.

"*Oh!*" she said. "Frank, he's cute! I want him! I'm going

to take him home with me! You hear that?" This last addressed to me. "We're fighting over you."

I smiled, wondering whether my IQ was not, at this moment, descending, like mercury in a barometer.

"Are you Jewish?" she asked me.

"Yes," I said.

"I told Frank you were Jewish," she said. "I said to him, 'He's either Jewish or Greek or Italian,' Can you tell what I am?"

"A girl," I said, "or a clever transvestite."

"Ooooo," she said, "you talk funny! What's a transvestite?"

"A man dressed as a woman," I said.

She made a mock attempt to slap my face.

"Ooooo," she said. "Did you hear what he said, Frank? Ooooo, I should slap his face! I'm a woman, a real woman, and proud of it."

Here she patted her bosom, which was very large and pushed very high so that it gave the impression of having been transferred from the headrest of an overstuffed chair.

"I'm half Jewish," she said. "Can you guess what the other half is?"

"Not unless you let me look at it," I said.

Another mock slap.

"Ooooo," she said, "don't get *fresh*. If you keep on talking like that you're gonna have to leave the table 'cause Frank and I are very respectable. Right, Frank?"

Frank rolled his eyes in a droll manner, moving the pupils from one corner to the other. I knew that it was a mannerism of current teen stars, but to me it looked like the mechanical eyerollings of Charlie McCarthy. I recalled, with a sense of wonder, that Boychick might never have seen Charlie McCarthy.

"How old are you?" I asked Frank.

This produced another eyeroll, or, more accurately, two complete cycles of eyeroll and the answer: "I'm nineteen. I'm just turned nineteen."

"Does he look nineteen?" said Florence. "I told him that if he told anyone he was nineteen they'd say he's lying. He looks about fourteen."

But that was not true. Frank was one of those people who have their middle-aged faces at birth, their childhood and adolescent faces appearing almost as interruptions. The youngness in Frank's life seemed a parenthesis inserted into the sentence of his life.

"You look eighteen or less," I told him.

This generated another eyeroll from Frank.

The two of them looked at each other as if they were sharing a wonderful joke. I was reminded of those pairs of characters (usually of the same sex, like Mutt and Jeff) who populated the cartoons of my childhood.

"How old are you?" said Florence. And then, "Don't tell me, let me guess," and she leaned forward for examination. "Ooooo, you got grey hairs in your head. Did you know you got grey hairs in your head?"

"Yes," I said.

"Oh, Frank," she said, "I bet he's an old man!" And then, patting my arm, "I didn't mean that. Did anyone ever tell you you were goodlooking? You know, I like you."

"I like you too," I said, which was a lie. To me, she belonged to a whole species of monstrous women. I could even remember the first one of that type I had seen, or rather, the first three. I was five-years-old and living on Kingston Avenue in Brooklyn. Behind the apartment house I lived in there was a concrete playground bordered by iron fences, not laminated steel hurricane fences, but old-fashioned iron ones, black, with a *fleur-de-lys* stuck on top of each stake. And those girls—how odd I can even recall the place!—they were congregated at the top of the steps that led down to the cellar. They were talking in those special conspiratorial voices that girls at the age of twelve and thirteen develop to such perfection.

I, approaching them, tried to draw up that impossible calculus that would show me some terms of equality with them.

"What are you doing?" I had said.

I had seen what they were doing. They were looking at each other's armpits.

"You're too young," one of them had said.

And then they had looked at each other with a Baroque slyness that only a Bernini could capture and lowered their heads until they were almost touching.

The third girl made some gesture that admitted me into their circle and I, in gratitude, showed them my five-year-old armpits, in one of which, I believe, there actually were three long hairs.

"Oh," said one of the Bernini faces, "that isn't real hair. That's just regular hair."

"What do you mean?" I said.

"It's a special kind of hair that grows there," she said.

"What's it like?" I said.

"I can't tell you," she said. And then she looked at the

second Bernini, whose mouth curled in a perfect, vicious laugh. To my astonishment, my protector joined in.

"Tell me!" I told my protector.

"She's right," my protector said. "If you were ten years older—"

"No, eight," said the first Bernini.

"No, ten," said the second Bernini. "A boy's got to be about three years older than a girl."

"Well, what would you tell me?" I said. "Why don't you tell me, and if I don't understand I'll tell you and maybe you can explain."

"We can't tell you," said my protector. "If we told you, your mother would come out and kill us."

"She'd chase us off the block!" said the first Bernini.

And the one I had named my protector threw back her head and joined in the hectic laughter of the others. I fled. One of them called after me, "Come back when you're older and we'll tell you," and another, "Don't tell your mother that we talked to you about it."

This odd conversation is one of my earliest memories. We moved away from that neighborhood into a better one when I was six and I cannot remember anything more about the girls, although, from the familiarity with which they had spoken to me and talked of my mother, I suppose that we had had other meetings before the one I have narrated.

I saw them again, years later, when I was scuba diving off Long Island Sound. I saw them after my first minute of descent. They had been transmuted into three spider crabs. It was the early evening when scavengers come out for food, but these three crabs seemed not to be hunting for prey but to be playing with each other instead. It looked to me as if they had formed a ring-around-a-rosie and were dancing to some perfect crab-music I could never hear.

Such a transmutation is, of course, improbable, but, after all, those little girls are as surely lost to me by time itself—the selves that then existed more lost than the Dead Sea Scrolls, the oxidation process of normal metabolism (called, in common parlance, "life") having consumed them quite utterly. They were about twelve then, and so, at this writing, they have reached the age of thirty-six, if they are, for that matter, still alive.

The first Bernini was a school teacher, married, and finding necessity pressing after having two children, has returned to school teaching again. Her husband is in the fur business and as I write this the phone in her apartment is ringing. A friend is going to ask her to arrange the loan of a fur coat to wear to her sister's wedding.

The second Bernini is—right now, oddly enough—in that same apartment house on whose cement steps I had spoken to her years ago. She no longer lives there but returns there to the dentist she and her family had when she was a child. The dentist is now with her mother, which mother is by this time quite senile. The Bernini—who was given the name Sheila (and who has named *her* daughter Feona)—is outside in the waiting room, leafing through the same blackhead-removing ads she had read as a child. She does not know that before the dentist will have adjusted her mother's bridge and returned it to her mouth, he himself will have died, his spirit moving at an altitude of 10,000 feet, following the course of the Hudson to Albany, there to ascend to the bosom of our father Abraham. (Such is the journey of all Jewish dentists who live in Brooklyn.)

And the third girl? My benefactor? She lives in the Bronx and is, of course, the mother of the black-tighted girl who is guitarist and money collector at the Bizarre.

"A penny for your thoughts," said the fat Florence.

Frank was bobbing his head up and down to "Nice 'n' Easy" and behind him, facing one of the walls, was a boy in denims moving his hips in time to the music. He was very tall. There was the suggestion of the praying mantis about his person.

"Ooooo," said Florence, "look at *him!* What does he think he's doing? What's he shaking? He doesn't have anything to shake!"

And she giggled a horrible giggle.

It was true that his genitals were not evident and true that in general boys in blue denims take the trouble to have them tight enough to make their privates noticeable, the usual basket (the scrotum this) resembling in its shape the burial mounds of the Neolithic peoples of Northern Europe—a fried sausage laid on top. Nevertheless it is quite conceivable that, unless some special effort were made, a male with genitalia of normal size could move his hips without making the crotch evident.

Florence had spoken loudly enough for the boy to hear, but if he had heard he gave no sign. He continued to face the wall, hold his beer bottle, smile, move his hips.

"Ooooo, he's so *fun-ny*," said Florence, again in her loud voice.

An older, white-haired, pink-faced man standing on the side turned at the sound of her voice and smiled.

"Ooooo," said Florence, "that grey-haired guy is smiling at us! Shall I ask him over? I bet *he's* fun-ny!" And then, "You wanna come and sit with us?"

He smiled and sat down.

"Do you like to dance?" said Frank, turning to me.

"Yes," I said.

"Were you ever at the May We?" he said. "I think I saw you dancing at the May We?"

"No," I said. "I did go to the Grapevine at 28th Street. They had two stories, the lesbians on the street level and the boys below in the basement.

"I used to hang out at the May We," said Frank. "But my boy friend didn't like it. He was a real butch. He didn't like fairies."

"What happened to him?" I said.

"We broke up," said Frank. "One of my cousins told him that I was carrying on with someone else. So he beat me up and left me. But I got a hold of that cousin and made an X with my nailfile right here—" and he indicated a point on his cheek below one eye. "I ruined him for life."

"She's a real bitch, that cousin," said Florence. "I'll show you a picture of her."

She brought out a fat wallet and showed me a color picture of three overly made-up women in evening dress.

"She's the one on the right," Florence said. "That's Frank's three cousins. They're all in drag. This was a big drag ball."

"Those are my three gay cousins," said Frank. "I've got three gay cousins."

The white-haired man had sat through this with a sweet smile on his face. "And what's *your* name?" Florence asked now.

"My name is Jim," the man said, "but my friends call me Jimmy."

The sound of his voice sent a shock through me. It was the very voice used in all the jokes about fairies (the comedian always brushing his eyebrow down with his little finger). But neither Frank nor Florence seemed to notice.

"Ain't that nice!" said Florence. "Well, Jimmy, we're your friends and we're going to call you Jimmy."

She introduced us all to Jimmy and laid a hand on Frank's and smiled at him and then at me, her features denoting such patent contempt and malevolence that I was surprised Jimmy didn't notice it and take offense. Perhaps his voice, which seemed to denote an arrest of intellectual development at some small-child stage, indicated to Florence the advantages that could be taken, the insults that could be levied with impunity.

I was very, very unhappy. I felt that I was truly in the presence of what the Psalms, not mincing words, call the Wicked. It was as if Frank and Florence were two dinosaurs in need of malevolence, needing to have parts of their body submerged in mud and ooze.

"Can I get you all a drink?" said Jimmy.

"We can pay for our own drinks," said Frank.

"The hell we can," said Florence. She smiled. "I'm drinking scotch and soda."

"No thanks," I said. "I've just gotten this beer."

Jimmy went for the drinks.

"Isn't he something!" said Florence. "He's a real queen."

"What do you do for a living, Jimmy?" she asked him when he returned with the drinks.

"I work in the *theater*," he said.

"And where do you *live?*" said Florence, winking at Frank.

"I live on 14th Street, on the north side of the street," he said. "I like to say that I live in the North Village. If I lived any further north I wouldn't be able to say I was in the Village."

"I live in a hotel," Florence said proudly. She mentioned a Broadway hotel in the seventies.

"I've got an idea," said Jimmy. "Let's all give each other our names and addresses and I can call you up and we'll all meet for dinner some night at my expense. We'll have a party. All right?"

"It's all right with me," said Florence.

"Sure," said Frank.

"I'm sorry," I said. "I'm very busy with my schoolwork and I'm not sure I'll have any free evenings."

"Oh," said Jimmy. "He doesn't want to go with us. But that's all right. We'll get together without him. Is that right?"

"Sure," said Frank.

"We'll have a *par-ty*," Jimmie said, "and if Leo doesn't want to come to our party, that's just too bad. We'll have a party without him."

"That's right," said Florence.

I went to get another beer, wondering what jobs Jimmy had been able to hold with his peculiar mannerisms, what salves against insult he had used through his fifty odd years. And yet, apparently, he had survived. Was it possible that there was some particular place reserved for the Jimmy's?

85

And what did he do with his time? At the end of the day what magazines could he read that would have meaning for him? What in the newspapers held his interest? What novels did he read?

I got my beer and waited in line at the bar to go to the toilet. While I waited, I managed to finish that bottle and order another, and when I came back to the table I was pretty woozy.

This wooziness I would like to use as an excuse for what I next did.

I told them about Boychick.

It may be that I really was so drunk at that point that I didn't tell the story correctly since Jimmy, who was the only person I can remember commenting on the story, said, "I wouldn't let anyone treat *me* like that. If someone has a meet with me and doesn't show—"

He made a gesture to show that the person was through.

I remember thinking that this simply did not apply to Boychick and myself, that Boychick had had no appointment to keep. But I didn't correct Jimmy.

And then he was leaving, saying, "I think we had a nice time. Haven't we had a nice time?"

"Sure," said Frank.

"I know," he said, this in his dreadful voice hinting of milk and arrowroot biscuits, "*I've* had a nice time and pretty Florence here had a nice time and Frank has had a nice time and I *think* that Leo has had a nice time, even though he doesn't want to admit it."

"I've had a very nice time," I said.

"I'm sorry that you don't want to have dinner with us some night," said Jimmy. "Well, goodby—"

And after another round of handshakes he was gone.

I went to the bar for another beer. Frank and Florence were still nursing their drinks. I suppose they didn't have much money.

I cannot recollect the exact conversation we had on my return but I think there were two subjects: the state of Sicily and Florence's marital status.

Frank, who was of Sicilian origin, told me that the idea that Sicily was poor was erroneous.

"The women in the towns all wear fur coats," he said. "Minks. And they have diamonds. My uncle was there a few years ago. He said all the women have fur coats."

"I don't think so," I said. "I read some articles by a man called Dolci and he described the general conditions as bad."

"He must be a Communist," said Florence. "Are you a Communist?"

"No," I said. "I'm a socialist."

"Oooooo," said Florence, "if I'd known you was a Communist I wouldn't of asked you to sit with us."

"I hate Communists," said Frank.

"He's telling the truth," said Florence. "Everyone in his family hates Communists."

And then, for some reason, Frank was showing me his ring. There were too small colored diamonds in it. His former boyfriend, the one who had beaten him up, had given it to him. I think the ring was offered as evidence of the riches of Sicily.

"I've got a diamond ring," said Florence, "but the diamond is so big I wouldn't go into a bar with it. It's an engagement ring. I was engaged."

"It's true," said Frank. "I met her fiance."

"He wasn't a Roman Catholic," said Florence. "That's why I couldn't marry him."

"Didn't you know he was a non-Catholic when you got engaged?" I said.

"Yes," she said. "But I didn't know that he'd been married before. When I found out I told him that I couldn't marry a divorced man because the Church is against divorce and that in the eyes of God he was still married to his wife. I'm very religious."

No sooner had she said this than she took a crucifix from her overstuffed bosom and put it (the crucifix) in her mouth. Then she looked at me for a long time out of the corner of her eye. Finally she turned to Frank and said, "He doesn't believe me. Tell him it's all true."

"It's true," said Frank. "I met the guy. He was a war veteran. He had only one leg."

"Frank!" said Florence, "That's enough. Now that he's no longer my fiance I don't think it's right to be personal about him."

"She's right," said Frank.

"I wouldn't mind being engaged to *you*," said Florence, linking her arms through mine. I glanced down at her cross, which had managed, by some miracle, to get out of her mouth and was now resting on her pigeon-breast. "Look, Frank, we're *engaged*. I'm sorry I didn't bring my engagement ring but it's so big I'm afraid to take it out of the house."

There was more talk.

My basic feeling was one of shame. I was repelled by the pair and ashamed by my feelings of repulsion. These were, after all, people like myself, only with a little less education.

But it wouldn't work. My only thoughts were of getting out and getting home. That curious woodenness that comes to the limbs after drinking had now settled into my arms and legs.

"Let's go to the Pam Pam," said Florence. "Is that all right with you?"

"Sure," I said.

"We'll all go to the Pam Pam and have coffee," said Florence.

"All right," I said.

But no one moved to leave.

The hi-fi jukebox was playing "Nice 'n' Easy" again and, once again, Frank was singing along, or, more curiously, framing his lips to the words, as if he felt it more proper that Frank Sinatra should do the singing.

"Ooooo," said Florence, "you got nice legs."

She was feeling my legs.

"Watcha got in your *pocket*," she asked. She was already going through my left-hand pocket, the one near her.

She brought out some items, I have forgotten which, and exclaimed in childlike glee over each. Her dumb-chorus-girl enthusiasm, like Frank's *Journal-American* politics, seemed to echo a past pre-dating her birth.

She asked if she could look in my other pocket.

"Sure," I said.

She giggled and rolled her eyes, and leaned over to take the items from my right hand pocket, among which was my money. (I don't carry a wallet.)

"Ooooo," she said, "you got nine dallahs!"

"Yes," I said.

She gave me back the coins.

"You can keep the change," she said.

"Thanks," I said.

"Let's all go to my hotel," she said. And then to Frank, "The two of us can sleep with him. We'll share him!"

I wondered if she was seriously suggesting such a project. My fear centered not on an invasion of my physical privacy but of my life. Florence had not touched my back pockets, which had my memo book and my address book (inside of which were my identification cards).

"No," I said, "I have to get home."

"Where's your home," said Florence.

I had already told her. I told her again.

"Let's *all* go home with Leo," said Florence.

"No," I said, "I have a landlady."

"Give us your address and telephone number and we'll call you up sometime and come for a visit," she said.

"But I don't want you calling or visiting," I said.

Frank's face fell. I was startled that he could be so hurt. It was almost as if he felt that I had deceived him.

"Oh," he said, "if that's the way you feel about it."

"Let's go and have some coffee," I said.

We got up to go.

"Could I have my money?" I asked Florence.

"I'll give it to you when we get outside," she said.

There was a policeman on the corner outside Frisco's. The snow had begun to fall, very slowly, in big flakes.

"They've got the fuzz out tonight," I said. I held the door for Florence.

She giggled.

"You don't like cops?" she said.

"Guess," I said.

Frank helped Florence through the door, putting his arm through hers. It was only when we were all outside and he continued to hold her up that I realized Florence was some sort of cripple. She was much more obese than I had imagined and it might have been simply that her ankles could not support her weight. At any rate she was a pitiful sight, stumbling through the slight drifts of snow.

She was giggling all this time, perhaps from embarrassment. Knowing the neighborhood she must have come from, I could imagine the taunts of the children through her youth.

I walked on her right side.

"Could I have my money back?" I said.

She giggled again.

"What money?" she said.

"The money you took from my pocket," I said. "Nine dollars." She stopped and opened her pocketbook and took out a dollar, which she gave to me.

"May I have the rest of the money?" I said.

"What money?" she said. "You only had a dallah."

A grin settled on her face like the printed smile on a Woolworth paper mache Halloween pumpkin.

They had begun walking again. I stood, looking back at the policeman on the corner and again at them walking. If she had been an agile girl, or even normally mobile, I might have acted, but the sight of her limping along so painfully, even with Frank's aid, wrenched my heart. I turned and walked in the other direction.

I found myself speaking aloud when I went down the subway stairs. The words I said were "What will Boychick say when he hears about this?"

W ERE YOU IN FLORENCE?" said
Mother. No, I said. "You would have liked Florence," she
said. "You know, I'm sorry we didn't take you with us."

"Now Mama," said Dad, "what's done is done. There's no
use crying over split milk."

"Let me see your teeth," said Mother.

I opened my mouth.

"Are those the ones he's going to put the caps on?" said
Mother.

"Yes," I said.

"When is he going to put them on?" said Mother.

"Wednesday," I said. "I think the final pasting in will
be on Wednesday."

"Do you have to give him the money before he puts them
in?"

"He's asking for it," I said.

"That's not the way I work it with my dentist," said Dad.
"I pay him half when he's begun the work and the rest after
he's finished."

A moment of silence.

"You know, Abe," my mother said, "I'll never forgive myself for not having his teeth fixed."

"They're being fixed now," I said.

"No," she said. "I mean the whole mouth, orthodontial work. Let me see your overbite. Bite."

I bit.

"You have an awful overbite," said Mother. "It looks like someone pushed in all your lower jaw."

"Please dear," said Dad. "It's no use crying over spilt milk."

"Let her complain," I said. "In any case my teeth are not split milk. Never were."

"All right," said Dad. "Excuse me for living."

"I came to get the check for the dental work," I said.

"I'll mail it to you," said Dad.

"Why can't you give it to me?" I said.

"I don't like to see you carrying a check for so much in the subway," said Dad. "Don't worry. I'll mail it to you. You trust me, don't you?"

"Yes," I said. "But I have to go now."

"You'll get the check in the mail Wednesday," he said.

"Leo," my mother said. "Let me see your teeth again."

I opened my mouth and bit.

"I'll never forgive myself for not getting your teeth fixed," she said. "If I could think that we could get them fixed now, I'd get them fixed and send you up to Grossingers."

"To get married?" I said.

"Why not?" said Mother. "You know, I saw a thirty-thousand dollar wedding last week. Wait, I'll show you the casket—"

She went out, half-hopping as she always does when she wants to hurry, and came back with a small, metal-worked box, rhinestones studding its four sides.

"Everyone at the table got a casket like this," she said. "And one person at each table had a gold card under her plate and that person could take the flowers at that table. And guess who got the flowers at our table."

"You did," I said. I stared at the box on the table.

"Right-o!" Mother said. "If I told you how large the basket of flowers was you wouldn't believe me. It came in a large basket. You could take the basket with you."

"So you took the basket with you," I said.

"We could hardly get the whole thing into the back of the car!" said Dad, holding his hand to his cheek.

"Leo, I wish you could have seen it," Mother said. "And there was something else I wanted to tell you. What was it I wanted to tell you?"

"Please dear," my father said. "I don't know what you wanted to tell him."

"Now I remember," said Mother. "The father of the girl offered them either thirty-thousand dollars or the wedding. So they took the wedding. You know why? They're not stupid. They'll get both! He's a rich man. Who does he have to give his money to if not them? They won't live in rags, believe me. Do you know what the boy is? He's twenty-six—"

"Two years younger than you," my father said.

"And he earns five-thousand, seven-hundred dollars a year," my mother said.

"Did he have nice teeth?" I asked.

"I didn't notice," said Mother. "But believe me, Leo, he wasn't as handsome as you."

"Well," I said, "maybe I'll get my teeth fixed."

"I'll pay for it," said Mother. "But believe me, I'd be *glad* to pay for it."

Outside a little girl was screaming, not from any emergency but from some minor crisis her years had made more urgent. She was wearing a skate, only one, and I could hear the sound of its measure on the pavement as it alternated with the silent measure of the step taken by the unskated foot.

"I have to go," I said.

"Wouldn't you like to see the news on TV?" said Dad.

"Not unless it's good news, which it never is," I said.

"You've got to know what's going on in the world," Dad said.

"Please!" I said.

Dad giggled.

"OK," he said. "I'm sorry. Excuse me for living. Have you written to that writers' place yet?"

"Yes," I said. "I told them I'm coming."

"I spoke to that radio writer I'm treating," said Dad. "He says he thinks it's a sort of beatnik place."

"It isn't a beatnik place," I said. "It's a former millionaire's estate. It's full of very respectable writers."

"Oh, that fellow doesn't know what he's talking about anyway," said Dad.

I excused myself and left, Dad giving me a few extra dollars, these much needed since that afternoon I had bought a month's ticket for the St. George pool. The ticket had cost ten dollars. That afternoon, Boychick had not been at the pool. . . .

H E WAS NOT AT THE POOL on Tuesday or Wednesday or Thursday.

On Tuesday I had gone from 6:30 to 7:30.

On Wednesday I went to the dentist at 6:00. I had not protested when the teeth were put in, although it had been painful. I was grateful to have them. I was at the pool by eight, stayed til nine.

Thursday I finished classes by 8:00 and was at the pool by 8:30.

There was my dentist, my classes at NYU, and the St. George Pool.

When I say that he was not at the pool I mean that he had not been at the pool when I was there. I was still playing Submarine, hoping to be there when he was.

Perhaps my judgment of the time was wrong. When I had left him that Friday at four o'clock, he had said he had to go home, eat supper, and go to work. Clearly then, his work was near his home and was after supper. Might it not be that he swam after school (which would be after 3 p.m., I supposed) and before he went home for supper, which would be about five?

That Friday I went to the pool at 3:30. That day I could not have gone later at any rate, since I was going to meet Ariela directly after my Sidney-Spenser class.

Boychick was not at the St. George when I arrived at 3:30. The fat man who had been with the Negro boy the night I had met Boychick was in the steam room, alone and naked. I went into the pool and began my laps.

It was then, or about that time, that I began to sing the Leo song. This is sung to the tune of "My Darling Clementine."

One-two-three and
One-two-three and
One-two-three and four and five
I'm in trouble
I'm in trouble
I'm in trouble
I'm alive.

And then sometime during this hour, I believe it set in: a peculiar and dreadful feeling of defeat. I didn't want to go to my Sidney-Spenser class, did not want to get up from the class, get into the subway and get to Corpus Christi Church (there to meet Ariela in time to witness an amateur performance of *The Family Reunion*).

Oh, the wave of non-wanting and non-acquiescence that came over me! But it was no use. I would go to both the class and the play.

Cheated/displaced. I felt cheated and displaced. Cheated of a life that I have never had (these thoughts while drying off in the St. George locker room) and displaced in this present world (these thoughts in the subway going to class).

I arrived early, taking my usual seat at the long table. Dr. Freedman would be seated at my left. At my right, as last week, was a young instructor from Brooklyn College. Today he had a very bad cough. From smoking, he explained as he lit a cigarette. He went on to tell me about Dr. Freedman.

She was—*brilliant*. I knew he would say that. I would rather have her smart, and making me smart, than *brilliant*. But this choice, of course, was not given to me.

"Brilliant," he explained, and often derisive of her colleagues, often to their faces. She had not been asked back to certain schools. At this point, Dr. Freedman came into the room. The young man stopped talking.

There was about Dr. Freedman a Katherine Hepburn erectness of the head, a constant display of tension, and—so odd—a sense of displacement, as if, reading Spenser merely for her pleasure, she had been summoned, as in our dreams we are summoned, to talk about him. So she had appeared—with tea-party graciousness—here at coffee-klatch NYU.

"I am sorry," she said, here a wry smile as if we had all spent our lives eating cucumber sandwiches with her at our country estates, "that we can't have an interval for coffee during the class. I am sure that there are many of us—" another smile here, this one skeletal, *à la* Pushkin's Queen of Spades "who *need* a cup of coffee about this time of day. I know *I* do." Here another smile to show that she felt we were equals and that such intimate confidences could easily be exchanged without any breach of decorum. "But apparently," a knowing smile here," we . . . must . . . do . . . without."

She held up her hands as if, in a lady-like and genteel manner, to split the seas and heavens.

"But enough of that," she said, "Now, we . . . will . . . move . . . on . . . to . . . Spenser. I *am* sorry that we won't be able to cover as much of Spenser as I, for one, would like to—this term. We will have to confine ourselves almost entirely to *The Faerie Queene*, an area which is by no means—" here she sighed and clasped her bony hands together "small, as I assume you have all found by now. I am very pleased with the way things worked out last week and I think we will continue with the same method, each of you preparing a recitation of about five minutes on a subject to be agreed upon—"

One of the students raised his hand.

"Will there be a paper?" he asked.

Dr. Freedman closed her mouth and breathed in deeply through her nose.

She then said (opening her mouth): "This *is* a graduate course and a paper will be expected, indeed—" a smile here "demanded."

Obligatory laughter from the class.

"It need not be long," she said. "Indeed, for my sake, I would prefer it to be short, about ten pages. Pee Em El Ay rules to be followed on all questions of punctuation, of course, and there should be no trouble about that since En Why You *is* Pee Em El Ay territory."

She smiled and the class laughed.

"No further questions. Good. Of course, when I said a *short* paper I didn't mean . . . a bad paper. I shall expect —you are graduate students, all of you—a good paper . . . adult, well developed, showing, I hope, some . . . thought and—" smile, "some work. You can, all of you, discuss your subject with me when you want to, but I have a very full schedule so that anyone who wants to speak to me will have to . . . *waylay* me after class."

She smiled. Laughter from the class.

"But enough of such technical details," she said. "Let us move on . . . to Spenser. Mr. Caine, have you prepared a paper for us this evening?"

"No, I had to—"

"Mr. Gerard?"

"I've some notes but they're not on the subject assigned. I became interested—"

"Mrs. Green?"

Mrs. Green was a married woman who lived in Washington, D.C., and came in each week for the course.

"Yes," said Mrs. Greene.

I hated Mrs. Greene.

"Mr. Ives?"

No answer.

"Mr. Ives?" said Dr. Freedman.

"Has anyone in the class seen, or does anyone in the class know, Mr. Ives?" said Dr. Freedman.

No answer from anyone in the class.

"I still have Mr. Ives' class card," she said, "and he is officially enrolled with us. If anyone does meet Mr. Ives, *please* tell him that I have his class card. Mr. Keller, *you* are here. Have you prepared a paper for us tonight?"

"I have notes."

"A simple yes or no will do, Mr. Keller."

"No."

"Miss, oh excuse me, *Mrs.* Kilpatrick.

"Yes."

"Mr. Kirk?"

"Yes."

Mr.—how do your pronounce it?—Mister *Klozen?*"

"You've pronounced it correctly," said Mr. Klozen.

"Mr. Klozen, do you have a paper for us?" said Dr. Freedman.

"No," said Mr. Klozen softly.

I resolved to say my "no" in a loud voice.

"Mr. Tsalis?" said Dr. Freedman.

"No," I said. I was loud.

Dr. Freedman did not raise her face from the sheet. I looked across her to the Irish commuter. He smiled at me. I put my glasses on and took a good look at him. He wasn't too bad looking.

"Is that Miss or Mrs. Wasserman?" said Dr. Freedman.

"Miss," said Miss Wasserman.

"Miss Wasserman?" said Dr. Freedman.

"Yes," said Miss Wasserman.

"Miss Wasserman," said Dr. Freedman, "we'll start with you this evening since, in our last session we began at the other end of the alphabet. Will you give us your paper?"

"I wasn't here last week," said Miss Wasserman, "so I

didn't know which canto you had asked us to write on so I wrote on Canto I, concentrating on Canto I.

"Perhaps we'll hear your paper later," said Dr. Freedman. "Mr. Keller, I don't believe we've heard from you. Oh, excuse me. I see you don't have a paper this evening."

"I have notes," said Mr. Keller.

"I believe a prepared paper is better for class presentation," she said. "Mr. Kirk, will you read us your paper?"

"I haven't done as much work on it as I'd like to," said Mr. Kirk, "the first half is written out but the second half is in notes."

"Well," said Dr. Freedman, "let's hear as much as you feel is adequately prepared."

Mr. Kirk began to read in such an impossibly flat, mechanical voice (more mechanical it seemed to me, than any mechanism) that one found oneself listening to its texture rather than to the words. What heartaches, backbreaks, impossible defeats, had engendered this odd rasping voice?

I looked around at the other members of the class, who looked, each of them, as if they had stepped live out of the pages of *Psychopathica Sexualis*.

There wasn't a single really handsome person in the class. The Irish commuter, the most handsome, had a bad complexion.

This was not true. I had not thought of myself. I am handsome.

Dr. Freedman listened to the madly droning voice of Mr. Kirk and smoked cigarettes, Parliaments, one after another, nervously, making no attempt to be, or appear to be, less nervous.

Mr. Kirk's paper was unbelievably bad. The subject, the Bower of Bliss, occurred in Canto xii, the last canto of Book ii, and it was soon clear that Mr. Kirk had not read the preceding eleven cantos and did not know what was happening in the twelfth.

The Bower of Bliss is, essentially, a place of vile enchantment, a fact that one could hardly miss since Spenser, in that very canto, calls it just that. And Mr. Kirk had missed the point. He reported on the Bower of Bliss as if it were a Garden of Eden. Dr. Freedman smiled, and smoked on.

"That's as far as my report goes," said Mr. Kirk finally. "I have notes for the rest. I was going to attempt a comparison with the island in Shakespeare's *Tempest*. I have notes."

Dr. Freedman smiled.

"That would have been very interesting, Mr. Kirk," she said. "And I think you have observed many aspects of the Bower of Bliss. It *is* an attractive place but Spenser presents other aspects too. He is . . . subtle, but they are . . . there. It is, to quote Spenser, 'The sacred soil where all our perills grow! (2. 12. 37). And 'sacred' here means cursed. Yes, the Bower is pleasant, but Spenser lets us know that its beauty is cloying, false. The Genius who guards the garden, whose 'Looser garment to the ground did fall,/And flew about his heels', is not the Genius of generation and soul, but of Pleasure. Again, Spenser let's us know again and again that the pleasures of the Garden are not of Nature, but of Art and that they are—even at first glance—cloying and unsatisfying. The flowers are *painted*, some of the grapes on the vines are of *gold*. Now, who wants golden grapes? And the two

naked girls playing in the fountain? Isn't there something—
well, of the striptease show about them? Notice that Guyon,
the knight of Temperance, is not completely inured to these
delights. 'His stubborne brest gan secret pleasaunce to em-
brace.' (2. 12. 65). It is the Palmer who saves him, draws
him back. Again, notice that there is too *much* harmony.
"Birdes, voices, instruments, windes, waters, all agree.' (2.
12. 70). Would one want such harmony in Nature?"

She shook her head.

"No," she answered herself.

The bell rang.

"Well," she said, I'm very pleased with the way our recitations have worked out. Next week we'll have Book III, which
treats Britomart and Chastity. Let us all try to get together
on the Masque of Cupid. That's in the House of Busirane,
Canto XII of Book III."

The class was leaving.

Mrs. Greene, the Washington commuter, stood up, waiting to talk to Dr. Freedman.

"Yes?" said Dr. Freedman.

"I found the Bower of Bliss very beautiful," said Mrs.
Greene in her special culture-voice.

"Well, of course," said Dr. Freedman. "It is beautiful but
compared to Nature's beauty it is . . . overdone. You and
I are not as close to Nature as Spenser was."

"Where were you brought up?" I asked Dr. Freedman.

Dr. Freedman turned away quickly as if she had not heard
the question.

I had observed this avoidance in her before, had guessed
that in some way she had broken from her home—with
English literature her bill of divorce.

Yes. Yes. Yes. That was the trouble, the real trouble. There was something as essentially false about Dr. Freedman's "appreciation" of Spenser as there was about Mrs. Greene's. They could not, would not, admit that Spenser's time had gone.

It was an admission that had to be made if one were going to gain an honest appreciation of Spenser. His art, resembling in some ways that of the late Italian Renaissance, was one that depended on a certain atmosphere. It was as if there had been a party and one was now picking up the costumes and paper horns and candy containers. They were of interest, these objects, but the party was over.

I left the classroom. Spenser was dead, his time gone. Gone his blonde females, their rent garments torn in flight from fiend, their snowy paps exposed; gone his Irishmen, his nightmare world, his castles, tortures. There had been something curiously lacking, almost claustrophobic in his vision. The same situations occurred continually in only slightly different forms, always the endangered maidens, the fiend (male or female or monster) and the rescuing knight. And that childish love of blonde hair, oceans of blonde hair tumbling down from the head of *every* heroine.

I walked toward the subway.

Spenser had had his party. I didn't mind picking through the costumes and tinsel, but I wasn't going to pretend that it was *my* party. . . .

My trick knee (right) came out the next Wednesday. I went down to the English Folk Dancing Society but could not dance. Ariela was angry at me but said nothing. I did not go with her to Brooklyn, went uptown, home, instead.

There was a slight snow on the ground.

I wrote Adam a short letter and got into my bed with its electric blanket. I was to finish the Gottfried von Strassburg *Tristant* and Chaucer's "Knight's Tale" before I went to sleep.

Outside my window, there was a scratching sound. I raised the blind. It was the vine that had grown up around a wire leading to a roof-top aerial. Amazing how this scratching sounded like the plaint of an animal.

*It's my first morning on the outside.*

*I've been interned for some time; I can't remember how long.*

*Adam and his wife insist I stay with them till I'm on my feet.*

*I'm a little embarrassed, not for them, but the children.*

*The middle girl—the one I hardly know, has, I suppose, elected to be my champion.*

*She's the only one home when I get up in the morning. She is in the kitchen, showing me where everything is, and then, seeing I want out, telling me the door's always open, showing me the walk beside the highway in front of the door.*

*I walk outside.*

*It's a strange grey-pink day (morning or evening?). The cars seem faster than I remember them, less noisy. I walk out and onto a bridge. Its rails, green-painted, stand like a vine against the pink sky.*

On the bridge a car is stalled and the driver is underneath fixing it.

I see his shoes, luminescent, by the car-edge, and know—how?—that it is Boychick.

He crawls out from underneath the car.

It is.

We stand facing each other. Cars whizz by. . . .

M<small>R</small>. T<small>SALIS</small>," said Dr. Freedman, "are you prepared to pursue Chastity for us this evening?"

The man beside me cleared his throat, sending his astral body through the ceiling

Mrs. X, the commuter from Washington, puffed on her cigarette. The paper in her pocketbook crackled sympathetically.

"I'd like to start at the end of Canto XI," I said.

"But you *will* get to the Masque of Love?" said Dr. Freedman.

"To it and through it," I said.

"Very well," she said, "begin."

So I opened my mouth and began:

"A young man is fleeing from Ollyphant the Giant—"

"Here," said Dr. Freedman, "we have but one of the many representations of bestiality. We must not forget whose brother Ollyphant is."

She opened her book and read:

For as the sister did in feminine
And filthy lust exceed all woman kinde

So he surpassed his sex masculine
In beastly use . . . .

Dr. Freedman smiled broadly. An air pocket, caught in her denture, escaped with the whinny of a newborn foal. Outside one heard the scream of a woman, followed by the sharp report of a gun.

"Proceed, Mr. Tsalis," said Dr. Freedman.

"Britomart, the maiden knight of chastity, gives chase and Ollyphant flees in fear—"

". . . he the flavor of chaste hands might not bear," said Dr. Freedman.

"At this point, Britomart comes on a weeping knight. It is Scudamour who is weeping for Amoret, his new bride, who, just after their wedding, was abducted by Busirane and taken to his castle."

"Spenser," said Dr. Freedman, "gives us some intimation that this punishment visited upon the couple is perhaps in some way connected with some . . . fault in their nature."

She had taken her pencil up and was tapping the table with it to indicate her complete absorption in the subject. I had not any intimation that Scudamour or Amoret deserved any punishment at all.

"Continue, Mr. Tsalis," said Dr. Freedman. She nodded as if I had been responsible for the interruption and that she, catching us all straying, had led us back to the path.

I drew in a deep breath. The Irish commuter across the way looked at me and smiled.

"Scudamour explains that the castle is surrounded by an impassable barrier of flames. But Britomart is able to pass the barrier. Scudamour, witnessing her success, tries to follow but finds that he cannot pass the flames."

Dr. Freedman put down her pencil again. She could put down a pencil more loudly than anyone I ever knew.

"Yes," she said. "Here we see Spenser indicating to us quite definitely that Scudamour lacks that chastity necessary to rescue someone from the house of Busirane."

She smiled like an addict after a fix.

"Go on, Mr. Tsalis," she said.

"Britomart finds herself in the outer room of the castle," I said. "The walls are covered with tapestries showing the transformations effected by love. We see Jove as a ram, thus transformed for love of Helle; as a bull for love of Europa; as a shower of gold for love of Danae, a swan for Leda, an eagle who snatches the Trojan shepherd Ganymede from the Ida hill. Apollo—in love with the fair Daphne, the lusty Hyacinth, the fair Coronis—brings death to each. We see Neptune as transformed into a steer for love of Arne, a dolphin for love of Melanther, a winged horse for the snaky-locked Medusa."

"Britomart sees a motto over the door, *Be Bold*, and then over the door to the golden room, *Be Not Too Bold.*

"She enters the Golden Room and there, when the clock strikes twelve, beholds the Masque of Love.

"Ease introduces the Masque and he is followed by min-strels, bards, rhymers, and then Fancy, a lovely boy like Ganymede. He is arrayed neither in silk nor satin but only in 'painted plumes . . . /Like as the sunburnt Indians do array their tawney bodies.' "

The room spun before me, I almost hearing Boychick's voice as he waved his arm at the pink neon sign of Katz's delicatessen across the street. "Three hundred years ago, he said, "there were only cowboys and Indians here." And then, the image of the brown Kewpie-doll Indians sold on the Coney Island boardwalk, their bodies a celluloid shell and around their loins bands of dyed chicken feathers.

"*Desire*, I said," comes next. He hold sparks of fire in his hand, and is followed by *Doubt* walking as if on thorns. His partner is *Danger*, who holds a net in one hand, a rusty blade in the other—one called Mischief, the other Mishap.

"Then Fear and Hope, this last a maiden dressed in silk with locks bound in gold. She is always smiling, sprinkling her favors in the form of holy water, 'and did great liking show/Great liking unto many but true love to feowe.'

"Then *Dissemblance* and *Suspect*, who holds a lattice before his face. This theme of the face hidden behind a lattice grating as the image of jealousy is developed at great length in Proust.

"Then *Greed* and *Fury*, the last with Pinacles, she naked and brandishing a firebrand.

"And after them *Displeasure* and *Pleasance*, the wasp and the honey-bee.

"Now Amoret enters, led by *Despight* and *Cruelty*. Her chest is cut open and from it her heart has been taken, which heart is now on a silver platter. It has been transfixed with a deadly dart.

"Then Cupid, the winged god. The cloth around his eyes is now unbound, and he is riding a lion he has tamed."

The Irish commuter looked at me and smiled broadly. He had wonderful white long teeth.

"Then," I said, "Reproach, Repentance, Shame, Strife. Then Anger, Care, Unthriftyhood, Loose of Time, Sorrow, Change, Disloyalty, Riotise, Dread, Infirmite, Povertie. And lastly, Death with Infamie."

My mouth had gone dry and the tears so filled my eyes that I could not see the page.

"This Masque of Cupid with Amoret—whose name, of course, signifies love—details as I see it, certain vital paradoxes of love. The theme of the pairs is, I think, essential. Although this is, of course, a *demonstration* of, quite plainly, the pains of love, Spenser is much concerned with showing their attachment to the pleasures. Thus, if there is Fear there is also Hope, if Doubt, Desire.

"And so, when Britomart, who is Chastity, rescues Amoret and takes her from the castle, the castle the emblem of the bondages of love, disappears. But with the castle, the lover himself as well."

After class I had begun the walk to Alys' apartment, stopping at an outdoor phone booth set between two warehouses to call Mother and wish her a happy Shabbos.

Mother was always polite during my Friday night phone calls. Years before she had been more demanding.

"Is anyone there," she had always asked. "Where are you?"

And I had said, "A telephone booth," winking at Frank who would be coming from the kitchen with two Tom Collins. The phonograph was playing the Folkways recording of the Bhagavad Gita.

Tonight I had called from a phone booth.

How far from Columbia, this world of dark and empty buildings—where now for some reason, on the second story of one, there was not only light, but through the large, old-fashioned, tall windows, the sight of a series of knitting machines going. There were no workers visible but only the moving spools of thread: red, gold, yellow, purple, brown, white, turning and winding, technicolor ghosts keeping endless traffic with eternity. I walked on past an Esso sign. It seemed to me that only some lack of faith prevented my turning a corner and finding, not a bum's hotel or shabby bar, but my friends, and even myself, waiting for myself upstairs, playing the Gita forever.

Dr. Freedman had returned the copy of *The Jews in the Renaissance* that I had lent her. Cecil Roth, the author, is a renowned English scholar. Accurate, often interesting in his choice of material, and always, unaccountably, boring. The chapter I had called to Dr. Freedman's attention was entitled "Among the Platonists in Florence," Dr. Freedman having pointed out the importance of Florentine Platonism in the work of Spenser. I thought that she might be interested in the Leone Ebreo, "Leo, the Jew," and his work, *I dialoghi di amore.*

At the corner past the factory with the sewing machines I stopped.

I decided not to see Alys that night.

I would go back to the West Side, to the Village proper.

Perhaps Boychick would be in Jim Akins on Sheridan Square.

I peered in the window.

He wasn't.

I walked on.

I passed the corner building where my friend Lenore had lived when she had worked for the correspondence division of Blue Cross ("We're going to teach you how to write a LETTER!"). I was just out of college and working as a copy boy for the *Journal-American* at South Street ("Boy!") and, covered with grime, I used to go to her house at night to take a shower.

Now three blocks beyond I passed the house in which Shel had lived when she returned to New York from New Orleans and had a job writing advertising copy. ("They get mad at you if you read," she had told me.)

So long ago. I was joining history.

I came now to Frisco's corner.

It hadn't been closed yet, though the newspaper had headlined the crackdown on gay bars, a season sport this, as legitimate as a fox-hunt. The *Daily News* headline read: ACT TO ALLEVIATE JOINTS WHERE THEY DEVIATE.

From the straight world, the straight press, not a word of protest.

Miserable, stinking cowards.

I peered in Frisco's window.

He wasn't there.

Somehow, I felt Frank and Florence wouldn't be there either.

I went in.

I stood there in the smoky room, not at the bar, which was too crowded, but away from it.

I noticed two boys at the bar. One was looking at me. He had the head of a stuffed panda. He smiled.

The smiles of gay boys are something special, and since it is the custom of the world to say only unpleasant things about homosexuals, I would like to mention here the richness of their smiles, the special resonance of their smiles.

First, they are gratuitous. They are not called forth by a joke, or an incident, by anything said or done. There is, to my mind, nothing like it except—not a smile, but a move —the opening move in chess and checkers.

It is a mirrored smile. One feels (justifiably?) that the mirror played some part in its genesis, that each gay boy in his gay mirror has met his face and smiled—a smile curiously less self-conscious than the one now presented to me as he tilts his head back, showing more rather than less eyeball, tooth, chin. An odd ritual, strangely dignified so that it reminds one of two elders of Bethlehem meeting at the city gate, one taking off his sandal to give to the other, this to validate the betrothal of the Moabite Ruth. In that gesture, the smile of the sleeping Boaz, the gleaning Ruth, the sweet and bitter Naomi-Mara. And such is the effect of the mirrored Moabite smile that, on beholding it, I have always found that I, as if mirrored myself, am smiling too.

The exchange of smiles, like the serve in tennis, is given only once.

It is the smile of the exit from Hades. "I am the returned and visible Eurydice," the smile says.

You glance in amazement at the smile, almost wishing to declare:

"But if you are Eurydice you could never return or, if you did, I could not behold you."

And the smile answers saying "Very well, I am a substitute for Eurydice." And then, more sadly, "No, I am Eurydice. But you are not Orpheus. It is only to Orpheus that I cannot return."

"Hi," said the smiling boy.

"Hello," I said.

He had a round face, round eyes like buttons, long lashes.

His companion turned around. He was a tall, very ugly Jewish boy, his only good feature being a magnificent, near-permanent smile that was quite a feat of bravado. His teeth were awful. He was later to have caps put on nearly all of them. I never saw the complete job but when I saw him that summer at Riis Park, all those large teeth had been filed down into stumps in preparation for the caps.

"You look *lost*," Howel said, he of the stuffed panda head and the Moabite smile.

"What do you mean." I said.

"Out of place," Howel said.

"You mean straight?" I said.

Howel laughed and rolled his eyes at the other boy who laughed and laughed.

"Oh," said Howel, "I didn't mean *that*."

"People say that *I* look straight," said Marvin.

"This is Marvin," said Howel. "He's the biggest queen in the forty-eight states."

"What do they have in Alaska?" I said, shaking Marvin's hand. "A mutant from the long nights?"

They both gave me a blank look.

"My name's Howel," said Howel, "with one 'l'. It's a Cornish name."

"What is it with two 'l's?" I said.

"I don't know," he said, "but with one 'l' it's Cornish."

"Don't be insulted," I said, "but I'm going to get a beer."

I ordered a beer. We moved to a table at the back.

They were drinking scotch and soda or something hi-class like that, and Marvin was congratulating me on having gotten Howel to talk to me.

"He never cruises," Marvin said. "I had to make him come with me tonight. He's not my lover."

"My lover left me," said Howel.

"He could have gotten *lots* of other lovers," said Marvin.

"Aw! Come on!" said Howel.

"What do you mean 'come on,'" said Marvin. "It's the truth. You should have seen him in the De Lys before."

"*Me!*" said Howel, "I wasn't doing anything!"

"I didn't say you were doing anything," said Marvin. "You were *being* done."

"Howel rolled his eyes at the ceiling, like Joan Crawford in *Our Dancing Daughters*.

"It's the truth! he said. "If we hadn't left in another minute I'd have called a policeman!"

"It was bumper-to-bumper," said Marvin.

"What's bumper-to-bumper?" I said.

"Ass-to-ass," said Marvin. "That means it's crowded. Haven't you ever heard bumper-to-bumper?"

"No," I said.

"I'll bet he's a virgin," said Marvin.

"Excuse me," said Howel, "I have to go to the bathroom." He got up and left.

Marvin took the opportunity of Howel's absence to tell me about Howel's former lover. Oddly enough, although Marvin had been playing footsy and kneesy with me (without any encouragement from me), while Howel had been present, he did not continue his suit now.

"He's a real bastard," said Marvin.

"Howel's lover?" I said.

"Yeah," said Marvin.

"Was he Jewish?" I said.

I stared at Marvin's lips, those thick, too-red, too-expressive Jewish lips, at Marvin's face, not pale so much as dark, unpleasant yellow.

"I'm ashamed to say he was Jewish," said Marvin. "He was such a bastard. You know what he did? He slapped Howel's face in front of everybody."

"Who was everybody?" I said.

"All of Howel's friends," he said. "Half of them were

straight. I could have fallen through the floor. Howel's heart was broken. This is the first night—no, the second—he's gone out since they broke up. His heart was broken. I thought he was going to kill himself. I mean it. Here he comes."

Marvin pressed my knee to indicate the return of Howel. When Howel sat down at the table, Marvin kept it pressed against mine.

"You really never been to the De Lys?" Howel asked me.

"Have you ever read Spenser?" I said.

"No," he said.

"Well," I said, "while you were at the De Lys I was at a Spenser class."

"Is that Spenser?" Howel said, nodding at my *Jews in the Renaissance.*

"No," I said. "It's a book I lent to the teacher."

"Oh!" Marvin said, "teacher's pet! You trying to make the teacher?"

"The teacher," I said (coldly—I have a cold voice), "is a woman."

"You should go to the De Lys," said Howel. "It's be-to-be there."

"I know," I said, "bumper-to-bumper."

"No kidding," said Howel. "Why don't you go to the De Lys?"

"Should I?" I said. "You mean now?"

"No!" said Howel. "Some other time. I mean, you've got good looks. You look like Tyrone Power around the eyes."

I took his hand.

"You want to take them home with you?" I said. "How about looking at the rest? There may be something else you want."

Howel laughed and laughed. Marvin continued to grin and increased the pressure on my knee to indicate his approval.

"Waiter!" said Howel.

Howel and Marvin ordered another round.

"How about you?" said Howel.

"Oh," I said, "I'd get drunk."

"So get drunk," said Howel.

"OK," I said.

"Where do you come from?" said Howel. "You sound English."

"No," I said. "It's real Brooklyn."

"You must have got that accent when you went to school," he said. "What school did you go to?"

"Columbia," I said.

"It is gay?" he said.

"No," I said, "very non-gay."

"I go to City—" said Marvin.

"And is *it* gay!" said Howel.

They both laughed.

I felt curiously light-headed in my old age and decrepitude, like the old man in the Chinese poems (there are so many!). Light-headed with a little wine, conscious of his shabby clothes, white hairs, few teeth, and then, curiously, free.

"If you come home with me," I said, "I'll shave and take a shower."

I laid my hand on Howel's.

"I'll even brush my teeth," I said.

I had passed into that happy state where victory or defeat would almost be one. I could see that Howel was going to accept.

"Look," I said, "you know I'm very drunk. I hope you're not expecting fireworks. I just want someone to sleep with."

"*I'm* willing," said Marvin, pressing his knee against mine.

I ignored him. "Will you?"

Howel shrugged. "Yeah," he said. He looked more like a stuffed panda than ever.

"I'd like to go soon," I said. "I'm awfully tired."

"We'll all go," said Marvin.

"I shouldn't have drunk this," Howel said. "I'm allergic. I've probably broken out all over my back. My skin's probably a mess."

And I, very dizzy, smiled at him, thinking how really odd it was that in this world of sex your flesh suddenly became an object to be presented. Almost, it seemed, as strange and distant to me as the flesh sacrifices of the Temple of Jerusalem.

And then we were all in Howel's car and driving into Brooklyn. There was an image of the Holy Infant of Prague on the dashboard.

We were driving along Eastern Parkway.

"Oh gosh!" I said. "This is where I used to live."

"The boy next door," said Marvin. "Just like in the movies."

But not quite next door. Howel turned to his right and went downhill, south, to that section of Brooklyn—or, rather, a section of Brooklyn—that I did not know at all. There were those little Monopoly houses like the ones I saw from the elevated train when I visited my parents.

Howel stopped the car and let Marvin off.

"Listen," he said, "I'll call you tomorrow at 12, hear? And be near the phone so I don't have to talk to your sister."

"Okay," said Marvin. And then, shaking my hand, "It's been very nice meeting you."

"Thank you," I said.

He closed the door and we were off.

Howel had turned the radio on while we had been going into Brooklyn and was playing it now as we went back. I asked him to turn it off.

"Wait!" he said. "They're playing my song! Oh! I love it!"

And I was crossing Brooklyn Bridge in the middle of the night and suddenly realizing that the driver was drunk.

"Can I keep the radio on?" he said.

"Sure," I said. "Just don't go over the side. I've only finished the first draft of my novel."

I slid down in the seat and looked at the night sky. The JEWISH DAILY FORWARD sign, lit up in neon, was visible from the bridge. Amazing they could still afford it.

We got off the bridge at Delancey Street, passed Ratners, several soda stands still open (EGG CREAM 12¢), news stands piled high with *Daily News* and *Daily Mirror*.

"Do you like the car?" Howel said.

"Oh, yes," I said.

I had not really noticed it, except that it was rich, new-smelling.

"I've got two cars," he said. "I gave the other to my sister because I wrecked it. I'm getting a new car."

"I'm so glad." I said.

"I gave one to my sister," he said.

I yawned. "That's very generous," I said.

"No," he said. "I'd smashed it and she had to pay for the repairs. I hadn't made too many payments on it, so what the hell, no skin off my ass."

"Sure," I said.

"What's the best way to go?" he said.

"Up the West Side Highway," I said. "Get off at 96th Street."

We went up the ramp to the driveway. On our left stretched the Hudson, on our right the signs, some of them madly archaic, painted even before my birth for products that no longer existed.

On our right, in the dock, waiting to go to sea, the *Isolde, Brangene, Helvig Torm.*

*The boat was the Vaterland, one of the Belgian Line (Blue Cross? Red Cross?). My father—then a boy of thirteen— had gone with his mother and two of his sisters, Fryma and Rivka. They were to join his father, who already had a grocery in Cohoes, a small milltown in upstate New York, near Troy.*

*At Odessa they had taken a train to Poland, to the city of Grodnow in the province of Briansk. At the German border the police had come on board to see that all the doors and windows were sealed for the ride through Germany. All the Russians were deloused. Later my father had stood*

*with his thirteen-year-old nose pressed against the car win-
dows, looking out at the fabled streets of Berlin, all regular
and straight, glistening and wet in the winter night. . . .*

*The boat trip took nearly ten days. My family was in
steerage, eating potatoes, herring, and borscht.*

*The representative of HIAS was there at the docks to give
them instructions and get them train tickets. They were to
go to Albany and from there to Troy, and there to wait all
night in the station until the local train came to take them
the three miles to Cohoes.*

*None of this was unusual. So many Russians were going
to America. He himself already had three sisters in America,
one married. Still, it must have seemed adventuresome and
daring and thrilling to him, just as it must be for some acrobat
when it is his turn to walk the rope.*

*What book was it that my father was reading that night
when he waited for the train to come?*

*And then in Troy, in the railroad station, who is it that
holds the piece of paper with the address in his (her) hands?
Is it his mother or himself who shows the piece of paper to
the stranger? And was it very cold that night? Did my father,
in his youth and the heat of expectation, not notice the cold,
or even, with a certain flair for drama, wish that it were
colder, that blizzards might whirl around them to emphasize
their journey-ness: "A pillar of clouds by day / And a pillar
of flame by night."*

*Was there a telephone? Had they phoned him?*

*And the house where they were to live—which was house,
grocery, and synagogue (the Jews in the town having bought
him the house so that the downstairs could be their synagogue,*

*he both rabbi and* shoichet, *slaughterer of kosher meat)—
is it warm?*

*And then they sit. They are drinking tea from glasses surely,
and then—this I know—my grandfather Leo whom I was
never to know, this other Leo, was telling my grandmother
of the daughters who had already come to America.*

*"And Lea," he said, "Lea already has a boychick!"*

*But the word boychick, a compound of the English word
"boy," and "chick," the Russian diminutive for "little," is of
course an American Yiddish word unfamiliar to my grandmother her first day in America. And hearing the word "boy,"
she associated it with the word "goy" and leapt to the con-
clusion (erroneous, it would seem) that Esther had found
herself not simply a little boy but a little goy.*

I T WAS TEN O'CLOCK two months later, and I was lying in bed dozing. This is a bad habit I can't seem to break. I know that if I doze off in the evening I'm going to be wide awake late at night, and then, for some reason, never studying but always—what? Doing something odd, usually walking (softly) downstairs and out for a walk.

I've tried keeping off the bed, but by nine or so something's happened, and, distracted by the something, I'm there.

And on this night the telephone rang. I got up from the bed and answered.

"Hello," a voice said.

"Hi, Howel," I said.

"Do you know who this is?" the voice said.

"Yes," I said. "I said, 'Hello Howel.' "

"This is Leroy," the voice said. "You don't remember me. The St. George pool—"

But before he had mentioned the pool the knowledge had come.

"Boychick!" I said. "Where are you?"

I clutched the phone tightly.

"I'm at home," he said. "I moved out. I don't live at home any longer."

"Well, what do you mean you're at home?" I said.

"I'm living with this kid," he said. "I used to know him at school. He graduated."

"Oh," I said. "Do your parents know where you are?"

"No," he said.

"You should tell them," I said. "You don't want them to worry."

There was a pause.

"I wrote them. They wrote back saying it was OK."

"What's your friend like?" I said. "The one you're living with?"

"He's OK," said Boychick.

"Well, what's he *like*?" I said.

"He's a little funny," said Boychick. "You know."

"You mean he's a fairy." I said.

"You wouldn't know it to look at him," said Boychick, "You know, he likes to dress up. He's a he-she."

"You mean," I said, "in women's clothes?"

"Yeah," said Boychick. "That's it."

"He sounds odd," I said.

"He works in the ladies' foundation garment section in Macy's," said Boychick.

"Are you lovers?" I said.

Another pause, like the working out of a problem in a mechanical calculator and then:

"No."

"Do you sleep in the same bed?" I said.

"Yeah," he said, "but we don't do nothing."

"Oh," I said. "I'm sorry. Well look, do you want to see me? What made you call?"

"Well, he said, "I remembered that you told me your phone would be connected in the middle of the month—"

"But that month was December!" I said.

Boychick laughed.

And suddenly I was afraid, terribly afraid that my harshness would drive him away.

"Oh, Boychick," I said. "I've wanted to see you so much! I was at the St. George swimming almost every day and I looked for you in the Village dozens of times!"

"I'll call you next Saturday," he said. "The kid goes out every Saturday night to a concert in Carnegie Hall."

"All right," I said. "Look, can you let me have your number?"

There was dead silence on the phone and then I heard Boychick talking to someone.

"Is someone there?" I said.

"It's the maid," he said. "I was just telling her what to do."

"Oh," I said. "Can you give me your number?"

Another pause.

"Don't you want to give it?" I said. "Oh, Boychick! I just really don't want to lose touch with you again! Don't you trust me? I won't use it unless I have to. Are you afraid that your friend will be jealous?"

"Yeah," said Boychick.

"Look," I said. "I promise I won't use it. Won't you give it to me?"

He gave me a number. It was an Ulster exchange. I wrote it on a piece of paper taped to the wall, an announcement of a writing contest at Antioch College.

"I'll be right off," Boychick said to the person in the room with him and then to me: "Look, I have to help the maid."

"Just a moment more," I said. "It's so wonderful speaking to you. Are we going to be meeting Saturday?"

"Yeah," he said.

"When will you be calling?" I said.

"Around four," he said. "Look, I gotta get off."

"OK," I said. "I'll see you Saturday."

It was only when he had hung up that I realized that ten o'clock at night was late to have a maid.

Then again, frightened with the lover's odd illusion that his wish, realized, must be so magical that it could only be illusion, I was grateful that the impossible, or highly improbable, had been realized, that Boychick had remembered me, had called.

I looked again at the number written on the wall, remembered his odd pause before giving the last numeral. Was that last number real?

Impossible to tell. I could have called the number at once, but it would have been a violation of trust.

THE WEEK went by quickly. It was nearing the end of the term. There were three reading lists, each a rival to the other, tacked up in my bathroom, I checking off each night which of the essential readings had been finished. My Spenser exam (which I considered the *dragon*) would be first, Friday; then my Anglo-Saxon exam; then easiest, nicest, the Chaucer.

That Friday, the twentieth of January, there was a blizzard and the Spenser examination was postponed until the following Friday.

I did not learn this until that night when I went down to NYU. One of the boys—men—in the class came over to me downstairs and told me he was sure they'd have to cancel the examination. I went with him to the magazine shop across the street and waited outside the telephone booth while he called the professor at her home.

It was even as he had predicted.

This was the first time I had really spoken to the man. He was younger than I, but already married and a teacher in Queens or at Brooklyn College.

Looking at him as he spoke, I wondered how his wife

could have married him with his bad complexion, his bad breath, bad teeth, slug-soul. Did she kiss him and in her mind transmute his earnings into furniture, linoleum, a modest winter coat for herself, and later, feeling his cock within her, think of the prospect of a child, its opportunities for carriage, diapers, playpen?

"Are you married yet?" he asked me.

*Yet!*

"No," I told him.

He went on to advise me to read Watkin's *Shakespeare and Spenser.*

"That has all the material you need," he said. "She doesn't really expect you to read the whole *Faerie Queene*. It's too long. We couldn't cover it in one term—"

I didn't tell him that I'd read the entire *Faerie Queene* three times.

He gave more advice and then explained to me the mechanics of his life, which consisted—I have forgotten exactly—of some kinetic equation about traveling time to two different schools with slight differences in salaries.

Going home on the subway, I tried to reflect on what keeps man to job, husband to wife, but, as always found the world unintelligible. I knew only that after these several years in New York City, there was, not in the entire city, a single person whose thoughts in any way centered on me, no one to whom I was really important. I had had friends at Columbia, but they were married, or insane, or busy. My only contacts with the world that I had known, of ideas, and of talk, were in my letters to Adam, my old straightnik roommate.

When I went to sleep that Friday night (the snow falling, not falling, falling again), my bed, that bed beside the window, seemed to change its position—not that I could feel it moving, but, waking or half-waking late in the night, felt that the foot of the bed pointed to the window, that the bed stood away from the south wall like the long perpendicular vertical or a T-square. And I found myself, in that sleeping-waking state, telling myself with great assurance that he would and/or would not come and/or call on Saturday.

He did not come. He did not call.

I could perhaps recreate those moments, that long chain of recurrent moments on Saturday when my hopes rose, fell, formed themselves around the memory of his voice, the business-like way in which he had remembered "the middle of the month." A moment later, I would remind myself of the other fact: that he had waited an extra month before he phoned.

And then—clear as a mother-of-pearl button—the beautiful fact: I had spoken to Boychick again. I had told him that I remembered him, which seemed to me the important message.

This was followed by another reflection—that Boychick had not been surprised, not in the least surprised.

It was 4:00 that winter day, then 5:00. At 5—I know this from a letter I wrote my friend Adam that day—he had not come. And then—in the letter (now returned to me by Adam at my request), I note that it was 5:15 and I had used the telephone number he had given me. I had dialed it. A man answered, youngish-sounding. I asked to speak to Leroy. He told me no Leroy lived there.

It was then that I was certain that Boychick would not call.

I say *certain* but this was not so.

My hopes revived several times during the night,—like one of Poe's lady corpses. I imagined any number of reasons why he should not call. It was snowing, he was sick, his roommate had stayed home, he was ashamed to call and say he could not come, his parents (mother and German step-father) had come and taken him from his friend's apartment and now had him at home, he sitting in the living room, listening to his stepfather's German waltzes on the phono-graph and unable to go outside and phone me.

And then I was overcome with the certainty that Boychick had, absolutely *had* tried to phone me while I, unfaithful, was on the phone and that somewhere at this moment, defeated, he was leaving the telephone booth of the candy store (rab-bit's foot and green transparent dice hanging uselessly from cardboard rack on the side!) and was walking, on unrubbered feet, through the snow-filled streets.

The last time given in the letter to Adam is 10 pm, but I think it was much later that I followed the resolution typed out, to take a hot shower, get into my electric-blanketed bed, and read Chaucer until I could go to sleep.

H<small>E'S GOING</small> down to Florida with a friend of his," I told Ariela.

"A boyfriend?" said Ariela.

"Not a lover," I said. "A straight friend. He has to see his draft board down there, I think. Then he'll be back in New York for an operation on his polynoidal cyst."

"Is this Boychick?" said Ariela.

"No," I said. "Howel with one 'l.' "

Ariela laughed.

She was leaving next morning for Palm Beach. We were in a taxi on our way to check her luggage at Penn Station.

"What about Boychick?" she asked.

"I haven't heard from him."

"He hasn't been at the pool?"

"No."

"Well, keep trying, honey. That swimming is putting a little red in your cheeks."

"Alys says it's love."

"I say it's exercise. If you ever get some money you should go down to Florida and get in some sunshine and birdwatching too. Maybe—what's his name?—"

"Howel."

"Maybe he can take you down to Florida."

"No, he's coming back here and going to work for a supermarket. I'm going to Yaddo in February—"

"You're not going to stay in the city and look for Boy-chick?"

"Ariela! I'm not crazy!"

She laughed and patted my back.

The taxi came to the station and we began to unload her bags.

When the things were checked in I asked her if she wanted me to ride back to Brooklyn with her.

"No, dearie," she said. "You go back home and try to do some studying. Take care and write me and I'll see you when I come back."

We kissed and I went into the subway and home.

By eleven I was in the bathtub. The phone rang.

I got out and answered it.

"Hello," the voice said.

"Hello," I said.

"Who is this?" the voice said.

"Leo Tsalis," I said.

"Who?" the voice said.

"L-E-O, T-S-A-L-I-S," I said.

"I'm sorry," the voice said. "Wrong number."

I hung up and went back to the tub. The voice had sounded familiar. It was like a young boy's Brooklyn voice.

The phone rang again.

"Hello," I said.

A moment of silence.

"I'm sorry," the voice said.

"This number is UN 4-2598," I said. "What number was it you wanted?"

"Your number," the boy said.

"Who was it you wanted to speak to?" I said.

Silence.

"I'm sorry," I said. I listened to the silence for a few more seconds and hung up.

It was only when I was in the bathtub that I heard in the words, "your number," Boychick's voice.

Again I heard the voice. It was the voice of a Brooklyn boy. "Your numbuh."

Had he thought it was someone else? Had he waited and waited all this time, trying out the number only to hear a voice that sounded totally strange? Or had he expected that I would recognize his voice?

I heard again, as I hear now, the hesitation, the moment of silence, and then his voice: "Your numbuh."

It was very cold that night, zero weather. Time was running out. I felt sure that it had been Boychick and that there would be no third call.

His voice had been so sad.

I lay in bed, reading the Kennedy translation of "The Wanderer":

Even in slumber his sorrow assaileth
 And, dreaming he claspeth his dear lord again
 Head on knee, hand on knee loyally laying,
 Pledging his liege as in days long past
 Then from his slumber he starts lonely-hearted

Beholding gray stretches of tossing sea,
Sea-birds bathing with wings out-spread
While hail-storms darken and driving snow.

The wind rattled the skylight in the kitchen.
It was his voice. I knew it. "Your numbuh." Yes. My
number.
Oh.

Friday. Two weeks later.
I came home, tired, happy.
The term was ended. I'd taken all the exams, handed in
the papers. Safe.
Now I would be going to Yaddo to write my novel, then
back to New York to finish my master's somehow.
Mrs. Katz, my landlady, had asked me to buy a five-pound
bag of sugar for her at the Key Supermarket. There was a
Special.
Howel had come back from Florida and was soon to enter
the hospital for this operation. I was to call him this evening
or next and we to go out. He was determined to take me
into the World.
"You've been living like a her-mit," he had said on the
phone.
I left Mrs. Katz's bag of sugar on her kitchen table and
began to walk upstairs to my apartment.
I could hear the phone.
I was sure—how?—that it was Boychick as I was coming
up the last flight of stairs. I unlocked the door and ran to
the phone.

"Boychick?"

"Leo?" he said.

"Who were you expecting?" I said. "Robert Taylor?"

He laughed, and my heart opened. It was like seeing a field of buttercups for the first time.

"What is it Boychick?" I said.

"Listen," he said. "I'm free this evening. Can I come up?"

"Sure," I said. "When will you be up?"

"What time is it now?" he said.

"Five-fifteen," I said.

"We'll be eating soon," he said. "I'm at home. I can't talk much."

"You mean with the boy?" I said. "The one who sells foundation garments at Macy's?"

"No," he said. "My uncle. Look. I can't talk now. I'll be through with supper early. I should be there about seven, seven-thirty, ok?"

"Sure," I said.

He hung up.

The waiting was torturous, and again I wrote a letter to Adam, noting the time, assuring him that the snow falling outside was very heavy, and that it was so cold, so terribly cold that I would not be angry if Boychick did not come, but only sorry if he did not call.

I told Adam (the letter is before me now):

"Am amazed that I do not feel worse, but for some reason, think I will hear from him again."

I DID NOT GO OUT the next morning. The snow that had begun the night before was still falling. The fall was not as heavy as the night before, but the thought of wading through the still-mounting drifts in my rubbers was enough to keep me in.

At 2:30 in the afternoon, the phone rang.

It was Boychick.

"This is Leroy," he said.

"Yes," I said. "I know."

"I couldn't make it last night," he said. "It was snowing."

"I know," I said. "I didn't think you would be able to make it."

"Listen," he said, "I'm at the St. George."

"Yes," I said.

"Can I come up." he said.

"Sure," I said.

"I'm with a friend," he said. "Can I bring him?"

"Oh, Leroy," I said. "Can't you say goodby to him at the St. George?"

'I don't think I should just leave him," said Leroy. "Can't I take him to your place?"

"Oh, Leroy," I said, "I couldn't do anything with him in the apartment.

"Oh," said Leroy. "I see. Well, he could leave afterward. I mean we'd only need a few minutes and then he could leave."

"You want to see him alone?" I said.

"Yeah," said Leroy.

"Well," I said. "Can't you go with him to his place and see me some other time?"

"There's people at his house," Leroy said.

I paused, trying to imagine a situation in which people might be at a man's house when he was not there.

Leroy interrupted my thoughts.

"He lives with his mother," Leroy said. "He's an older guy. He gives me money sometimes. You know."

"Oh," I said.

"Can we come up?" said Leroy.

"Yes," I said.

"OK," said Leroy. "We're leaving now."

He hung up.

Now, alone in the apartment, I wondered what was going to happen. I was fearful, my largest fear being that I was to be taken advantage of, that Leroy's friend was also his mentor, that, hearing of me, he thought me a good prospect for some type of extortion. Would they rifle the room I gave them, taking valuables (*what* valuables?), or perhaps some personal document, some letter or card I would not

142

miss until much later? Or would they simply state that they would beat me up or make a rumpus and call my landlady if I did not give them money? I imagined Leroy's friend not as an "older" man but as another kid, in his twenties at most. He would do the talking while Leroy sat on the side looking embarrassed and smoking a cigarette.

I was frightened. I felt very much alone. If something happened, my life would never be the same again. Mrs. Katz would be shocked, but, while it lasted, she would stand by me for to her they would be the upsetters, the trouble makers. But afterwards, she and Shlomo would look at me as part of a mess. I would have to leave. They might even ask me to, but that would be unnecessary.

Of course I realized that I could quite simply tell Leroy and his friend, when they came, that I had changed my mind. But I knew that I would not do it, that there was something in me that assumed—falsely?—that Boychick, that Leroy, had been telling me the truth, that he simply wanted my apartment for the use of the bedroom. So many trap-doors had opened up under him. I would never provide another. It seemed important to me, the idea that each of us is a link, and that each time one of us lets go, as I was tempted to do out of fear, something, somewhere—often someone—was lost.

But *in my house!* If I could only get them a room somewhere! I telephoned the St. Marc Arms, a rooming house near Columbia where I had lived years before. There was no answer.

I called Alys and told her what was happening. "Alys,

I've very rarely asked you for a favor, but I'm asking you for one now. Will you come up here, just get in a taxi and come up?"

"I don't have enough money for a taxi," Alys said. I'd have to wait until Joycelyn gets back and ask her if she has some money."

"I have money," I said. "I'll pay for the taxi. Just come up."

There was a moment of silence. "Alys?"

"No," Alys said quietly.

"Thank you," I said.

I hung up and then took the phone again and telephoned the St. Marc Arms. The number was now busy.

I went into my bedroom and looked for anything that might possibly be handled or stolen. There were Adam's letters in a bundle in the top drawer of my dresser. I ran with them to the closet in the living room and put them on the shelf. Back to the bedroom and picked up all my blank checks and my check book and put them with Adam's letters.

I telephoned the St. Marc Arms again. No answer.

The buzzer for the downstairs door rang.

I went to the door and buzzed back.

It seemed like an age before I could see anyone coming up the stairs. I hoped that, as in "Monkey's Paw," my wish had been enough to make my visitors vanish.

But I heard their footsteps on the stairs.

Boychick appeared first, looking much as he had that day months before. He was smoking his cigarette and he gave me a conspiratorial wink.

I looked behind him at his companion.

The man *was* older. He was wearing a peaked ski cap and his hair was completely white. His face was a sort of Spam-pink and his mouth was set in a fixed, puppet-like grin.

On one point my mind was at rest. This man, I felt, was not an extortionist. He was a fool.

I let them in.

"Where shall we put our coats?" said Leroy.

"You can hang them in the closet," I said.

"No, no," said Leroy. "They're wet. Let's put them outside."

"OK," I said. "You can put them on this chair."

I indicated the sling chair in the living room.

"No," said Leroy. "They're wet. Let's hang them in the bathroom."

I gave them hangers and they hung up their coats. The man put his ski cap on the bath tub edge.

I went into the kitchen. They loitered in the hall. Leroy looked into my bedroom.

"I guess you want to use the bedroom," I said.

There was not another word said. Leroy went into the bedroom, the man followed, and the door closed behind them.

In the kitchen I could hear the sound of shoes falling to the floor.

I stood there, dizzy, feeling like Lizaveta, her head streaming from the ax blow.

I walked into the living room and looked at the phonograph, wondering if I could play a record.

The phone rang.

It was Alys, apologizing for having said no, and then discussing her reasons for it, the primary one being that she felt people were asking for too much from her and that she had to say no. She then went on into a long digression, the chief point of which was the fact that if someone imposed on her in her own home (apparently by simply staying too long) she was less able to say no. Conversations with Alys usually resolved themselves into examinations of the curious aspects of her general paralysis, an analysis for which she seemed to have the energy of a female Henry James.

I thanked her and said I understood. I was sorry, when I hung up, to be left alone again.

I went into the hallway. There were loud sucking sounds coming from the bedroom.

It was ten to 4.

I went and knocked at the door.

"How about you kids trying to finish soon?" I said.

There was silence. Then Boychick spoke.

"What?" he said.

"Do you think you can be out soon?" I said.

"All right," said Boychick from inside.

Then I heard the sound of the bedspring moving quickly. I was filled with shame, making them hurry for no reason, and yet I could not keep myself from feeling terribly cheated and cut off. I found myself walking up and down the hall with heavy footsteps, ashamed at this awkward threat to their privacy.

Finally the door opened a crack.

I could hear Boychick's conspiritorial whisper. When he

came out he was wearing his shorts and a T-shirt and went into the bathroom. I could hear a flow of urine hitting the toilet bowl. I was again filled with embarrassment at having these inner lives in my hands and treating them so harshly.

The door opened and I motioned Boychick into the living room.

"Whew!" he said. "I'm tired. I'm pooped. Look, I'll come Sunday, tomorrow. I promise."

He folded his hands in front of him and, like a child saying his prayers, held the small clenched fists together.

"When I promise," he said, "I always keep my promise. I *promise* I'll call tomorrow."

"Oh, Boychick!" I said. "Boychick, you don't have to promise. You don't have to call if you don't want to."

He stared at me.

"Oh, Leroy," I said. "You shouldn't have brought him here. It made me feel so bad."

"I'm sorry," he said. "I knew I shouldn't have."

"It's OK," I said. "It's over. Just try to stay a few minutes. I'd like to see you."

"OK," he said.

We turned to go down the hall as the man, fully dressed, went toward the bathroom.

Leroy and I went into the bedroom. The light had been turned on.

He sat on the bed. He framed the word "blackmail" with his lips, nodding in the direction of the bathroom.

"What do you mean?" I whispered.

"He knows my uncle," said Leroy, "so I have to go with

him. He knows about me. He saw me coming out of the hotel once with a guy."

"The St. George?" I said.

Leroy nodded. "He works in the towel room."

"What do you mean by blackmail?" I whispered and looked around to see if the man was coming back.

"He's gone," said Leroy.

As he said this I had the sudden conviction that Leroy was not being blackmailed or anything like it, that he had in fact some arrangement with the man to meet him outside.

I also felt, was nearly as convinced, that Leroy had arranged that the man would take something with him, something they would be able to use later. But the nature of the suspicion was such that I had to dismiss it entirely.

"How does he blackmail you?" I said.

"He can tell my uncle," said Leroy.

"Your uncle?" I said.

"Yeah," he said, "I'm living with my uncle."

"What happened to your friend?" I said.

He shook his head. "I had to move out," he said. "I had to live with someone over eighteen."

He made a derogatory gesture toward the bed.

"Wasn't he any good?" I said.

"He was disgusting," said Leroy.

"What did you do?" I said.

"We just lay there and talked," said Leroy. "He just talked."

"Didn't you do anything?" I said.

"He blew me," said Leroy. "Once, no twice."

"He didn't get in your ass?" I said.

"No," said Leroy. "I tried to do it to him but he said he had rec-something trouble. Is that the right time?"

"Yes," I said.

"I've got to get on home," he said. "It's a long trip. If I don't get home for supper—"

He made a gesture of a gun being put to his temple.

"You know, the telephone number you gave me that night wasn't correct," I said.

Leroy looked astonished. "It's—" and here he gave a number that was exactly like the other except for the last digit, which was now a three. It had been a four.

"Come into the kitchen," I said, taking him by the hand.

We went into the kitchen where I showed him the number on the piece of paper taped to the wall near the phone.

"I lie," said Boychick, shaking his head. "I lie all the time. I have to. My uncle's suspicious. You know why I couldn't see you last night and the time before that? My uncle wouldn't let me out of the house."

"Couldn't you have called me?" I said. "I mean, Leroy, it was pretty hard, just waiting and you not coming or anything."

"I *couldn't,*" he said, "with *them* sitting all around the phone."

"Well, you could have phoned this morning," I said, "before you met your friend."

He considered this for a minute.

"You're right," he said.

I didn't go on to pick out the other inconsistencies in his

story, among them the fact that the number he had given me as his friend's he now gave as his uncle's.

"Come and sit on my lap," I said and we walked back to the living room.

He sat on my left leg.

"Do you like me" I said.

"Yeah," he said, "but not like—"

"I know," I said. "Leroy, do you think of me as someone special?"

"Sure," he said.

"How?" I said.

"Well, you're different, that's for sure," he said.

"How?" I said. "How am I different? What's special about me?"

"You got a lotta books," he said. "You could open a public library."

I got up, and we stood close together.

"Maybe that's it," I said, holding his hand.

"I got to get dressed," he said.

"OK," I said.

He dressed and went into the bathroom and combed his hair.

"Do you have a plastic bag?" he said. "I want to put my bathing suit in it."

"I probably have," I said, "but I never know where I put things like that."

"It's OK," he said. "Just a brown paper bag. I don't want to spoil my coat. Everyone praises my English sporting coat."

I gave him a brown bag.

"Let me look at you," I said. "I wanted so much to look at you again, to see you. What school do you go to?"

Leroy hesitated for a second, several seconds and then folded his hands in that gesture of cherubic supplication.

"Please, please don't send anything to my school," he said.

"What's wrong?" I said. "Are you in trouble at school?"

"No," he said. "But I'm trying to get clear. My uncle's suspicious."

"I can't write to your house," I said.

"No," he said. "All my mail is forwarded to—" and here he broke off his sentence.

"Anyway," I said, "if I did write you, they wouldn't find anything but a drawing of the goblet with *Trist* and *solde* on it," I said.

He smiled.

"I read that book," he said.

"Oh?" I said. "What was it about?"

"There were these three guys," he said, "and they've got it in for Trist—"

"Tris-tan," I said.

"Tris-tan," he said. "And then there's this girl Isol—"

"Isolde," I said.

"And the other one, Isolde of the White—" he drew another blank.

"Isolde of the White Heads," I said.

"Yeah," he said.

I looked at him, wondering again if I would ever have been able to know what or how much to expect from him, if I could have been able to tell the story to him and make it meaningful. Enchantments, voyages—love, strong, hopeless, inevitable as death. All those mysteries, it seemed to me, which I had been closer to when I was sixteen than I was now.

Leroy was telling me about a guy he sees each Friday night.

"He's got this crazy place, see, real beatnik-like and he's got this liquor cabinet and we drink."

"Do you make it with him?" I asked.

A pause.

"No," said Leroy.

"Lie down with me for a second before you go," I said.

Leroy lay down on the studio cot in the living room, folding his legs. His shoes were well polished. He was wearing his overcoat.

I looked at his amber eyes and, closing mine, rested my face against his. His skin was very soft and smooth and smelled of perfume. I wondered if the smell was of hair tonic. I kissed his cheeks and when he raised his head (I think to prevent me from disturbing his hair, I kissed his chin. There were golden bristles on it.

"You're getting a beard," I said.

"I shaved it this morning with my electric razor," he said.

I kissed his nose and wondered if I should try to make him stay longer, wondered if my breath smelled good to him.

"I got eyes for you, Boychick," I said.

"Come on," said Leroy, "I gotta go."

We got up and Leroy went to inspect his hair in the bathroom mirror.

I followed him.

"Did the guy give you any money?" I said.

A pause and then, "No."

"I'll walk you downstairs," I said.

Leroy's rubbers were on a folded newspaper beside mine in the hallway on the ground floor.

"I'm sorry I didn't go to that movie with you," said Leroy.

I stared at him.

"*Exodus*," he said.

I remembered then having mentioned it to him at the time of his first visit. "Oh," I said. "I saw it. It really wasn't good."

Leroy gave me a conspiratorial wink and nodded toward Mrs. Katz's closed door to indicate that the conversation had been for her benefit.

"I'll walk you to the subway," I said.

"You don't have your coat," he said.

"It's ok," I said.

We went outside. The snow had stopped. It was a beautiful day.

"That guy's a stoop," said Leroy.

"You mean your friend?" I said.

"Yeah," he said. "He's got nothing up there. He tried to get a room at the St. George giving a false name and they asked for identification. He ought to know that every hotel asks for identification."

I didn't tell him that most hotels do not ask for identification.

When we neared the subway entrance, Leroy said, "Can I ask you for fifteen cents for the subway?"

"Sure," I said, and I gave him a five dollar bill.

"Is this your food money," said Leroy, "cause I would never forgive myself if I found out it was your food money."

"No, it isn't," I said. I bought two tokens. Boychick looked startled and, I thought, annoyed.

We went downstairs to wait for the downtown train.

"I'll ride with you down to 59th Street," I said.

Boychick sighed. "I'm going to Long Island Sunday," he said. "I forgot. I won't be able to call you."

"It's all right," I said.

"Look," he said. "I'm in this too deep. I've got to get out. Something's going to break. I think my uncle suspects. Let me just try to cut everyone off for three months. You're going away. When you come back, I'll call you or write you and we'll see each other again."

"Baby," I said, "you don't ever have to see me again if you don't want to. I love you. Don't worry about it. Whatever you want to do is OK."

He took my hand.

"I'll always think of you as a real friend, Leo," he said. The train came.

When we went inside, Leroy said, "Everyone's looking at you. They all think you're crazy, with no coat on."

"I don't care what they think," I said. "You're the only person in this car whose opinion matters to me. I thought you were going to be such a beatnik and rebel and now you're worried because I don't have a coat on."

Boychick smiled.

"I'm a conformist," he said, "a complete conformist. He looked toward the end of the car.

"Do you see the guy? There he is." he said.

"Who?" I said.

"The old guy I came with," he said.

"No," I said.

I thought you saw him in the station," Leroy said.

"No," I said. "How is it you didn't mention him?"

"I thought you noticed," said Leroy. "Maybe he was just waiting and no train had come."

"I doubt it," I said.

"I don't want to talk to him," said Leroy. "He's a creep."

"What will he want to talk about?" I said.

"About how you took our using the apartment," Leroy said.

"If you don't want to talk to him," I said, "we'll get out at the next station and wait for the next train."

Leroy hesitated (why did he hesitate?) and then got up with me at the next stop and we stood on the side watching the train pull out.

"There he is!" said Leroy. "Don't you see him? There!"

I didn't see him.

"He was sitting at the window," said Leroy.

I felt some pity for the old man. I could almost feel him at the window, pink-faced and childlike, all the fright of rabbit, doe and sheep showing in his stupid face.

And I, was I not kin to him?

"I gotta stop going to that pool," said Leroy, shaking his head. "Why do I keep going to that dirty hole?"

"The pool is not a dirty hole," I said. "I guess you've got quite a fan club there."

"You're telling me," said Leroy, and then, lifting each arm alternately, "Hi, Leroy! Hi Leroy!!"

He paused and shook his head.

"I think my uncle knows what's going on," he said. "He's so suspicious, even of my real friends—"

The train came.

"If I'm caught," said Leroy, "it will be either training school or back home."

"Are you on probation?" I said.

"No, I'm off probation," he said.

He had forgotten that the last time he talked to me he had said that he'd never been on probation.

The train now came to 59th Street and we got off.

"I'll wait for the express with you," I said.

"Everyone's looking at you," said Leroy. "Aren't you cold?"

"I'm always ten degrees warmer when I'm with you," I said.

Leroy looked around uncomfortably. Two women a few feet away were talking and one of them was looking at me.

I wondered if Leroy was more sensible than I.

"Look," said Leroy, "You know where I wish you were, over there—" he pointed to the opposite platform where an uptown local was just closing its doors.

Before I was forced to accept his invitation, his train had come in.

I waved at him as I ran up the steps.

I called Howel that evening to tell him about Boychick.

He couldn't see me at once because he was going to a new gay bar with Marvin but he would come up later.

He called back at 1:30 and was with me by 2:00.

I had washed the sheets in the machine in the basement and taken a shower and shampooed my hair. When we got in bed, I cried and hiccupped for a half-hour or so and then it was better.